PRESERVING THE FLAME

BY
COLIN BURBIDGE

Published in 2008 by YouWriteOn.com

First Edition

Published by YouWriteOn.com

Front cover photograph: Captain Victor Gough, Somerset Light Infantry 1944.
Rear cover photographs: Untersturmfuhrer Werner Helfen, Schutz Polizei 1944,
                           and Captain Gough.

CAPTAIN VICTOR GOUGH

I never knew my uncle Vic; he was murdered in the Erlich Forest near Gaggenau on 25th November 1944 together with five comrades from the SAS, four American airmen, and four Frenchmen. Their deaths might have gone undiscovered but for the determination of Major Eric Barkworth leading the SAS War Crimes investigation team. This is their story.

During the planning for D-Day it was recognised that the French Resistance would have a major role to play, following the initial invasion. They would be required to rise up in considerable numbers, commit multiple acts of sabotage, use hit and run tactics against the Wermacht, and generally make a nuisance of themselves by delaying the movement of arms and equipment, thus tying down substantial parts of the German army which would then become unavailable for front line duties.

To do that, the Resistance would need to be organised, directed, and supplied. The Special Operations Executive already had expertise in this area with their network of agents in occupied France and elsewhere. It was logical that SOE should be tasked with setting up a clandestine organisation to oversee the conduct and direction of an essentially guerrilla campaign, today they might well be described as "military advisers". Their solution was the "Jedburghs," a Special Forces group of some 300 volunteers from units of the British, American and French armed forces; and in addition a small number from Holland, Belgium and Canada. The idea of the Jedburghs came originally from Brigadier Colin Gubbins who in summer 1943 would become the Head of SOE. In July 1942 he wrote the following note to SOE's Security Section.

"A project is under consideration for the dropping behind enemy lines, in co-operation with an Allied invasion of the Continent, of small parties of officers and men to raise and arm the civilian population to carry out guerrilla activities against the enemy's lines of communication. These men are to be recruited and trained by SOE. It is requested that "JUMPERS" or some other appropriate code name be allotted to these personnel"

In March 1943 this idea was tested using eleven, three man "Jedburgh" teams in an operation codenamed "Spartan" which supposed an Allied invasion force was moving northwards from Salisbury Plain towards the East Midlands. As a result of exercise "Spartan" in April 1943 the Planning Section of SOE submitted a paper "Co-ordination of Activities behind enemy lines" to the Supreme Allied Commander, which recommended that:

> *"The methods of employment and control of resistance groups formulated herein be accepted and that general approval be given to the provision of the necessary personnel and stores so that planning may commence immediately"*

The experience gained from this exercise led in December 1943 to the formal go-ahead for recruiting and training a targeted 300 Jedburgh personnel by April 1st 1944. This figure was in practice never achieved. The purpose of Jedburgh teams, as defined in the Basic Jedburgh Directive of 20th December 1943 was:

> *"to provide a strategic reserve for creating and controlling offensive action behind enemy lines on and after D-Day where existing communications, leadership, organisation, or supplies are inadequate, and for carrying out additional specific tasks demanded by the military situation The principal function of JEDBURGH teams is liaison with resistance groups. They will be sent only to areas where there are actual or potential resistance elements, well behind the German front lines (at least 40 miles). They will be sent particularly to groups which need special outside assistance, or to which specific D-day tasks cannot be assigned until the last moment."*

All volunteers undertook a three part training course, providing they survived an extensive interview regime by psychiatrists. Preliminary training began in remote areas of Scotland, followed by intense practical courses. Radio training was undertaken at Fawley Court near Henley. From February 3rd 1944 the "Jedburghs" permanent training base, under cover of an all-purpose code name "Allied Commandos", was established at Milton Hall near Peterborough, family home of the Earl Fitzwilliam. US Jedburgh Sgt.Robert R.Kehoe remembers his time there:

"This was a great English Estate with a rambling old mansion from the 1700s. It could have been the setting for a Thackeray novel. One easily imagined supporters of the Stuart pretender roving secretly through the dark corridors within. The main house was used for administration, recreation rooms and a lecture hall. The latter had been the mansion's grand hall; its walls were covered with portraits and paintings – family treasures from another era.

A memorable experience during these months was provided by the series of "Jed Lectures" held in the Great Hall. They included talks by specialists on military tactics, demolitions and sabotage and the enemy order of battle. Some of the most interesting dealt with the situation in occupied Europe: economic conditions, the political scene and what little was known about security and counterintelligence. Much attention was given to the French Resistance movement, but there were large gaps and much outdated information. It was later, in France that we became aware of the strong political biases of many of the Resistance forces and the serious antagonisms within the Force Francaises De L'Interieur"

Here at Milton Hall they undertook several months of rigorous training including, concealment, ambush, demolition, armed and unarmed combat, and killing by stealth, in addition, they would need to be skilled in, ground-to-air signalling, organising reception of airborne supplies and living off the land, all hundreds of miles behind enemy lines. Many had never jumped by parachute before, that training being undertaken at Ringway Manchester. The teams initially comprised an English or American leader, the number 2 would be a national from the intended target country, and a radio operator would complete the trio. The radio operator was a crucial link to HQ, skilled in high speed morse and ciphers, adept in using shortwave radios like the "Jed-set" and B2 equipment, and able to effect repairs in hostile conditions. One key difference between the Jedburghs and other clandestine operatives was that they would be dropped behind the lines in full military uniform and not in civilian clothing. The eventuality of Jedburghs being captured had been considered by SOE. There had been proposals to provide teams with a false cover story but this was not carried through.

7

The briefing notes for the very first team "Hugh" despatched on the night of 5th/6th June 1944 read as follows:

"If Captured The team took no cover story with it to the field, so in the event of being taken prisoner they would be taken as soldiers in uniform performing their ordinary duties. Every established law of warfare would apply to them and they would give their name, rank, and number only."

Between June 1944 and VE Day 1945 Jedburgh teams completed 101 operations, 93 of which were with the Maquis in occupied France. Captain Victor Gough, (*code name "Arran"*), was leader of Team "Jacob", (the 26th "Jed" team to be sent into France) with him would go Lt. G. Baraud (real name: Guy Boissarie) (*code name "Connaught"*), and their radio operator Sergeant Kenneth Seymour (*codename "Skye"*). Both officers carried 100,000 Francs and 50 dollars and Seymour 50,000 Francs and 50 dollars. Victor Gough already had some knowledge of what to expect, for he had been a member of a shadowy group known as "Auxiliaries" who were selected to form a British "Maquis" had Germany invaded, with secret arms dumps and stores hidden throughout the counties of England. These "Auxiliaries" were nominally part of the Home Guard, and were developed by Colin Gubbins later Head of SOE. Their role would be to wage classic guerrilla warfare against an invading army. A few of them were later recruited into the Jedburghs and some 300 went on to join the SAS Regiment, once the immediate threat of invasion had evaporated.

Victor Gough was born in Hereford in September 1918; and attended Hereford Cathedral School from the age of 6 until 10, when the family moved to Bristol. His education was completed at Temple Technical College in Bristol which he left in 1935. After a short marriage, Victor and Edna May Gough divorced in January 1944. At the time of his mission he was billeted with a Mrs K. Baird at Ashfield House, North Petherton in Somerset. It is unclear what the relationship was between Gough and Mrs. Baird, she was 13 years his senior and still married, however he thought highly enough of her to enter her name on his SOE personnel form as his next of kin, and made her the executrix of his will. It would seem that Gough and Lt.Baraud were friends as well as comrades, because Baraud's personal effects were left at Ashfield House before their mission and later sent to Lt. Colonel Carleton-Smith (DR/JED) at Baker Street by Mrs Baird in May 1945. Lt. Guy Baraud was born in Bordeaux in 1914 into a large family (4 more brothers and a sister). Before the war he trained as an Insurance Inspector and before volunteering for SOE had served with the French Army in Morocco. In civilian life Victor Gough was a mechanical engineer with W.D. & H.O. Wills the cigarette makers in Bristol and had also trained as a draughtsman. He was something of a cartoonist which skill he continued to practice even during his brief time as a German captive. He had transferred from the Somerset Light Infantry to SOE in late 1943 as a training officer, before switching to operations in early 1944. His artistic skills helped him to win a competition to design the Special Forces wings which the Jeds wore.

Team Jacob was to parachute into France along with SAS Team "Loyton" from 2 SAS Regiment. They were ordered to place themselves at the disposal of Colonel Grandval (code name Planete) as liaison officers to help arm, train and organise up to 7000 FFI in the local region in as clandestine a manner as possible. No large groups which might attract enemy attention were to be organised and open offensive action was to be avoided at all costs, they would also carry out joint missions with SAS Team Loyton. Their orders also clearly stated that "Jacob" was to remain under the command of Etat-Major des Forces Francaises de l'Interieur. EMFFI was founded on 1st July 1944 as a joint command between SOE and the Free French based in Bryanston Square near Marble Arch. Another team from 2 SAS, Team "Pistol" would be operating in the Alsace region at the same time, tasked with specific demolition objectives.

Their destination was largely to be their downfall. They were to be dropped into the Vosges in Alsace, not just inhospitable terrain, but somewhat inhospitable inhabitants. The dome-shaped mountains rise to their greatest heights north of Belfort Gap and then spread westward for more than 40 miles toward the Moselle Valley, and northward for more than 70 miles parallel to the Rhine. They form chains of granite in the south and of red sandstone in the north, which fall abruptly to the Rhine

Valley; but to the west the forested slopes descend more gently. The highest Vosges summits exceed 4,000 ft in the region southwest of Strasbourg; which was to be the drop zone for "Loyton" and "Jacob" teams, and the higher peaks are covered with snow for nine months of the year. The steeply wooded hills afforded good cover for the Maquisards who tended to favour hilltop, log built camps, with tables, benches, sleeping cabins, and barricades, where the Tricolour could be flown in daylight. John Hislop in his book "Anything but a Soldier" described them as *"seeming as if they had been lifted straight out of one of Fennimore-Cooper's books"*

On the night of 12th/13th August 1944 two aircraft took off from RAF Fairford with the advance "recce" group from SAS Team "Loyton" led by Captain Henry Druce and SOE Jedburgh team "Jacob" under Captain Victor Gough. Their dropping zone was Le Mont near La Petite Raon some 300 miles beyond General Patton's advancing US Army. Captain John Hislop of Team "Loyton" recalls the drop in his book "Anything but a Soldier"

"......About 2 o'clock in the morning the dispatcher aroused us with the warning that soon we would be over the D.Z. He passed round a bottle of rum for anyone who cared to take a swig. Nervous excitement drove away the last tentacles of sleep and fatigue. The dispatcher walked down the line checking each man, which was a wise precaution since somehow, Henry Druce's static line had been passed through his parachute harness. Had this not been discovered he would have been suspended indefinitely and irrecoverably beneath the aircraft after he had jumped.

The plane had been coming down gradually as we approached the D.Z. till it was about 800 to 1000 feet, when the pilot began his run-in.

As we neared the D.Z., a clearing in a valley bounded by wooded hills, the blaze of the guiding fires on the ground came into view I remember wondering whether the Maquis hadn't overdone the illuminations – they looked like bonfires on Guy Fawkes night – and speculating on the possibility of the Germans seeing and investigating.

The plane sank lower the engines changed tone and the pilot began his final approach. The red light changed to green, the dispatcher shouted "Go" and like pins in a bowling alley the first group vanished through the floor of the fuselage.

By this time I was trembling with excitement and tension, as I stood jammed between the man in front and behind – the tighter we were packed, the quicker we were out, thus lessening the chances of dropping outside the area of the D.Z. The sense of claustrophobia blended with suspense and discomfort, which cannot have lasted more than three minutes, seemed interminable.

The plunge into the night air and the brief soothing caress of the slipstream as it twirled me about, was as refreshing as diving into a cool stream on a hot day. This illusion was dispelled immediately by the opening of my parachute and the start of my descent. Meanwhile the illuminations were getting nearer and, added to the bonfires, so it seemed was enough noise to wake the entire German force in the Vosges. As one of the Maquis let off a firearm either out of exuberance or by mistake (a far from infrequent occurrence as we were to find out) it crossed my mind that the enemy might even be among the reception committee. Another couple of seconds and I crashed through the branches of a sapling and landed gently on my back in undergrowth. Before I could rise a Maquisard appeared and helped me to my feet. Out of breath and in my best school French I spluttered the pass word, but for all his interest I might have been quoting the starting prices at the last Plumpton meeting. All he wanted was a cigarette, the parachute material and any items of equipment for which I had no further use"…

A six hour march then ensued before the parachutists would reach their hilltop rendezvous with "Maximum" and his group of about 100 Maquisards. The drop was not without its casualties. Captain Druce was concussed, French SAS officer Robert de Lesseps burned his hand on the cord paying out his kitbag, and Sergeant Kenneth Seymour of Jedburgh team "Jacob" sprained his ankle and fractured a big toe, which injury would within 4 days lead directly to his capture. In addition the "Jed's" wireless set was broken on impact. Captain Gough team leader of "Jacob" would now have to rely on the use of the SAS transmitter.

The task of working along side the local Maquis would prove to be much more difficult than London might have imagined. In this most Teutonic area of France, the majority of the population spoke better

11

German than French, and temperamentally they inclined more towards the inhabitants of Baden-Baden than to the French. This would have a significant effect on the creation of a resistance culture against the Germans. On the western side of the Vosges there was active resistance, but on the eastern side there was virtually none. This background would produce numerous denunciations and many collaborators. Due to the previous inability to make daylight drops in the Vosges no Maquis groups were founded until the summer of 1944, when a few isolated hilltop camps were established. However these groups were poorly disciplined and the actions of a few hotheads attracted German attention

The 1940 frontier between Alsace and the rest of France was also the dividing line between the responsibilities of Befehlshaber der Sicherheitpolizei France led by Helmut Schlierbach and B.D.S. Alsace. The man in charge of B.D.S. Alsace was Dr. Eric Isselhorst, a lawyer who had joined the Gestapo in 1935. An intelligent man he was considered weak in character and ineffective. These failings allowed a triumvirate of his Deputy Wilhem Schneider, Hstuf. Julius Gehrum, and Kriminalrat Alphonse Uhring to run things more or less as they wished. Schneider a former sea captain was pompous and fond of the bottle. Dr.Isselhorst referred to him as *"A drunken old trottel"*. Schneider's great friend and advisor was Uhring on whom he was said to rely heavily. Hstuf. Julius Gehrum was known to be extremely ruthless and even fonder of drink than Schneider. Isselhorst in his sworn statement to Major Barkworth described them thus *"Schneider was the figurehead, Gehrum provided the executive force, and Uhring the brains"*.

The German Army presence in the Vosges area was represented by Lt.General Willy Seeger and his 405 Reserve Division. A mixture of raw untrained conscripts and convalescent soldiers discharged from hospital. Their duties were the protection of important installations in Alsace particularly against the threat of heavily armed parachutists. It was not part of the Wehrmacht duties to deal with captured parachutists.

At the beginning of August 1944 Gauleiter Wagner gave orders for the construction of a fortification line on the western slopes of the Vosges. The working parties for this project were mainly drawn from the

Hitler Youth, whom the Gauleiter felt needed protection from the Maquisards. Dr. Isselhorst was ordered to provide extra police cover to fulfil this duty. To do this Isselhorst brought in a number of unsavoury Einsatz Kommandos. These groups of between 10 to 40 men, usually named after the group's leader were made up of some very unpleasant characters, including the dregs of the German Police and Wermacht, mixed with Moroccans, Azerbaijanis, Mongols from Asia, and low life French criminals.

From his sworn statement to Major Barkworth dated 14th November 1945, Wilhelm Schneider recalls how they were alerted to the presence of parachutists:

> *"As a result of a report received on 15th August from a Sicherheitspolizei unit that Maquis camps were being set up in the hills of the French Vosges, between the Donon and Raon l'Etape a conference was held at Schirmeck camp. I had been ordered there by my superior Dr. Isselhorst as he was going away to Berlin, and wished me to be at the central point to direct action against the Maquis. At this conference, this report was discussed. It originated from a woman of the Plaine Valley who had quarrelled with her husband, a Maquisard, and we assumed that she wished to be revenged on him. In the report was the news that English soldiers were with the Maquis, and the noise of aeroplanes had been heard at night. It was decided to call for re-inforcements from the Ordnungspolizei, Gendarmerie and notify the Wehrmacht. All these units received orders to investigate this report. As the presence of the Maquis and suspicious activity was confirmed, I was obliged in Isselhorst's absence to call in further re-inforcements and start the pre-arranged plan,*

> *The first sweep, East to West, was made by the Wehrmacht commanded by Generalmajor Kirchbach from Allarmont. They found nothing"*

The British parachutists and the Maquis they had come to organise would feel the force of this sweep for weeks to come. By September 1st the triumvirate (Schneider, Gehrum, and Uhring) had launched "Action Waldfest" Part1 when the Kommandos stepped up their pursuit of the "terrorists". By the time "Action Waldfest" Part 2

13

had been completed at the end of October virtually all Maquisard activity had been eliminated, never to recover.

Something else the British parachutists faced was the existence of a secret order from the Rechssicherheitshauptamt (RSHA) to the effect that all Allied military personnel, whether in uniform or not, who were taken prisoner during an action with terrorists (Maquisards) should themselves be treated as terrorists and therefore executed immediately. Dr. Isselhorst (B.D.S. Alsace) was given the order by Gruppenfuhrer Muller of AMT IV. After consulting with Gauleiter Wagner and General Willy Seeger, Dr. Isselhorst issued the order but with a rider, that clear evidence proving the prisoners had been associating with the Maquis, must be shown in each individual case before execution could be carried out. In a number of cases later investigated by Major Barkworth of 2 SAS, the Germans did not bother to establish this critical evidence and summary shootings occurred, sometimes being recorded as "shot whilst attempting escape" thus absolving them from producing any evidence whatsoever. It was against this backdrop that team "Jacob" and "Loyton" would be required to operate.

Radio communication with SFHQ was a key element of the operation and had to be carefully planned to specified schedules. Team Jacob's transmission times, (known as "skeds") were:

Odd days	0830 to 0900 hrs & 1300 to 1400 hrs,
Even days	1100 to 1200 hrs & 1700 to 1730 hrs
Night transmissions	2300 hrs and 0300 hrs.

The Maquis insisted that transmissions took place well away from their base camps for fear of the Germans finding them with radio detection equipment. Operators were required to travel with a guide 5 to 7 miles from base, each time in a different direction, in order to "talk" to SFHQ. "Jacob" Team leader Captain Gough sent his first message to SFHQ on August 13th 1944.

"Landed safely. Skye (Seymour) damaged ankle. Fit in 7 days. Am using SAS operator. Have contacted Maximum who is trying to contact Planete

for us. Are with Maquis group 2 kms south of Vexaincourt in Valley Celles-sur-Plene"

For 3 days Captain Victor Gough of Team "Jacob" and the officers of Team "Loyton" held meetings with the Maquis, drawing up lists of their requirements for arms and ammunition. The Maquis fed the parachutists on a simple diet of bread, cheese and dried meat, supplemented with the British rations. Some feel for the conditions in which Captain Gough and his comrades had to work, can be gained from his brief radio messages sent to SFHQ.

15th August "could not get radio contact yesterday. Sent message blind. Expect conference with Maximum and Planete today. Must march 5 miles from camp to send messages. Can only manage 1 sked per day at present"
16th August "Maximum and Planete not arrived yet. Maximum has 800 men, 600 are sedentaire. Only 60 armed. More news after conference"

But on the 17th of August everything was to change.

Kommando Schoner numbering about 30 men had been based at Chateau Belval for only one day when they were ordered on their first sweep on August 17th. Their commander Erwin Schoner had prior to the war lived in the United States where he worked in New York. He spoke English with an American accent and it is almost certain according to Sergeant Seymour's 1945 de-briefing report that Schoner was one of the Gestapo to interrogate him. This was the day that Kommando Schoner would take two British prisoners. Sergeant Kenneth Seymour was the first. What exactly occurred depends on which version you believe, and the fate of the first two British prisoners could not have been more starkly contrasted. Early on the morning of 17th August the British parachutists and their Maquis hosts were alerted to approaching German troops of the Wehrmacht 405 Division led by Major Reiser together with Security Police Kommando Schoner.

The evacuation of the camp proceeded in single file down steep hillside paths. Because of his foot injury Sgt. Seymour was carried on a makeshift stretcher by four Maquis. In his report on Phase 1 of Operation Loyton, SAS Captain Henry Druce describes what happened:

> *"After about 400 yards we bumped into a German patrol who were eating. We retreated and got off the track. Unfortunately one German who saw the last man in our column shouted "Achtung" whereupon he was shot by the man he had seen. (It later transpired that we had been betrayed, and our position sold to the Germans by one of the Maquis, his name and particulars are held by Capitaine Jean Serge). The patrol seemed about 30 to 40 strong, so at first I decided to attack them, but within a few minutes shouts were evident from their reinforcements further up the path. Fearing the enemy would soon be on the lower path also, I decided it best to make for the R.V. in small parties as I was not keen on risking our necks for a few Germans. Unfortunately this meant leaving Sgt. Seymour to be taken P.O.W. for he still could not walk"*

When firing began his French bearers dumped Seymour on his stretcher on the ground and fled into the forest. In the next few days rumours spread amongst the Maquis that Seymour had a) shot himself, b) been shot by the Germans, or c) been bayoneted to death. In fact Seymour was captured alive by Kommando Schoner and taken to their base at Chateau Belval. Very early the next morning he was transferred to Schirmeck camp. In his sworn statement of 14th November 1945 Wilhelm Schneider states:

> *"Seymour had been brought in, in the morning and another English prisoner who wore the same uniform as Seymour arrived some hours later. He looked younger than Seymour and looked stronger and more athletic. He had short blond hair and a healthy fresh complexion. He was placed at the entrance of the camp, like Seymour, but about 6 metres away from him"*

Seymour was placed on a small platform near the camp entrance and remained there for some 6 hours. This second arrival was Parachutist Hall of 2 SAS team "Loyton". Seymour denies seeing him although he was well placed to see all the comings and goings at the Camp. Hall did not co-operate with his captors. He was ostensibly taken away by van to Natzweiler Concentration Camp nearby, but on route was taken out of the vehicle and shot.

Sergeant Davis of team "Loyton" was the next to be captured. In his book "Anything but a Soldier" Captain. John Hislop SAS, whose radio operator Davis was, described him thus:

"He was a tall, lean athletically built young man, intelligent, responsible and absolutely reliable. He had a somewhat cynical outlook on life, possibly on account of an impediment in his speech, but was a man of sterling character and an excellent soldier."

On the 18th August following a skirmish with German patrols, Captain Hislop's team retreated at great speed. Sgt.Davis the radio operator became detached from the team and lost his bearings, easily done in the steeply sloping hillside forests. On Sunday 20th August at St. Jean le Sauley, Davis was refused food by a farmer and was seen talking to the village priest Abbe Colin who promptly reported him to the HQ of Kommando Schoner, who picked him up. In the same statement Wilhelm Schneider tells of interrogating Davis:

"The third prisoner was brought in by Schoner.I got this prisoner to write his name for me. He wrote in block capitals DAVIS. He was tall and well built. He would not tell me where his home was, but said he was a railway clerk before the war. He refused to say where he was born. I told him that he would be treated as a Maquisard for being with them, in accordance with the instructions we had received. He replied "my country right or wrong, I am a soldier and I have to do my duty". I told him he must prove to me that he was a soldier, for he had no pay book or identity discs which he could show me. At last he produced some pennies from his pocket as proof he had come from England. He would answer no military questions. I admired his attitude which was in great contrast to that of Seymour. I was so impressed by his soldierly bearing, and his impassivity when told he would be shot as a Maquisard, that I made representations to Isselhorst, that this soldier should be treated as a POW and sent to an appropriate camp, instead of being treated like a Maquisard. Isselhorst at first said his hands were tied and that they must all be shot, but later said he would see what could be done"

Schneider also said that among numerous parachute containers the Germans had found in the forests, was one containing personal mail for the SAS men. Schneider claimed that he handed over two letters addressed to Davis unopened. Notwithstanding Schneider's intercession with Dr. Isselhorst, Davis was later taken into the woods in the hope of showing the Gestapo where the Maquis equipment had been hidden, and when he refused was shot.

Meanwhile Captain Gough's radio messages tell their own story.

26th August" Arms, ammunition, grenades urgently needed for 600 men. Can take maximum of 70 containers. Send also Jed set, 2 rucksacks. Area getting hotter daily"

5th September "Have no W/T set. Contacted SAS team Loyton here. Got them to arrange arms drop on Pedal with you. Could not receive arms – were attacked on DZ – many casualties. Team Loyton having resupply drop here in few days. Please contact them and send me rucksack and further 100,000 francs. Food difficult"

6th September "Do not drop on Pedal tonight. DZ in Boche hands. Liaison with Maximum excellent until battle at Leon. Trying to contact him to reorganise".

15th September. "Skye (Seymour) captured 17th August. Reported shot as reprisal 20th. Please check with Red Cross. Connaught (Baraud) killed. I am now sole member of team Jacob. 100 maquis killed, 100 captured in same battle. Rest dispersed."…

16th September. "Maximum OK but unable to operate. Huns watching him. Have rallied 200 maquis and armed them with arms given by SAS. Transmitter and receiver you sent both broken on arrival. Think can manage by using SAS set. Chins up"

18th September "Have contacted 800 maquis under Marlier. Sent message with SAS yesterday for arms drop. Gave ground. SAS will liaise with you. Great difficulty working alone. Can't come up on regular skeds. Will come up on emergency channel when can. Have not had money yet. SAS having personnel drop to team here tomorrow. Please send money addressed to me with one of their officers"... ...

That was to be Captain Gough's last message to SFHQ. They continued to send him messages until 28th September 1944.

The Maquis had become almost unmanageable. The following incident on August 29th 1944 was typical of the indiscipline of the Maquis groups. Colonel Maximum's group captured two young Milicien prostitutes, aged 15 and 16. They were brought to the hilltop camp but security was so slack that the two girls were able to walk out without challenge. As a result they spent the next few days touring local villages with the Germans identifying any men they had seen in the Maquis camp. The very next day August 30th 1944 the SAS Diary records another debacle.

"A Frenchman called Fouch was found near the camp and brought in for interrogation. He claimed he was in the woods looking for mushrooms. At 19.00 hrs a messenger arrived to say there was to be a parachute drop that night. At the drop zone one container exploded on landing and another pannier burst on impact. Whilst the containers were being collected (and looted) by the Maquis, the prisoner Fouch snatched a Sten gun and tried to escape. His guards who were Russian, and whose common language with us and the Maquis, was German, shouted "Achtung". The French thought we were being attacked by the Germans, started firing in all directions, or fled. Eventually Fouch was re-captured and was shot by Lt.Baraud (Jed Team "Jacob") at point blank range. (His body had vanished when Lt.Baraud went back next morning. Afterwards it was said Fouch had been wearing a bullet proof waistcoat).

Most of the containers had by now been looted by the Maquis. One Frenchman died from over-eating looted rations, another died of a stroke after eating plastic explosive, and another was wounded by a bullet during the melee".

At the beginning of September the main party of Team "Loyton" led by 2 SAS C/O Lt.Colonel Brian Franks with 23 men parachuted into the Vosges. Their landing proved to be a shambles as rival groups of

Maquisards arrived at the Drop Zone, plundered the containers, helping themselves to weapons and ammunition until they began to fight over their spoils. On September 6th Major Dennis Reynolds and 14 more men arrived, after which Brian Franks ordered a move well away from the troublesome groups of feuding Maquis.

The SAS aims and objectives for Operation "Loyton" did not always mesh with those of Special Forces H.Q. The Jedburgh team "Jacob" took their orders from EMFFI, a joint Anglo/French Command and it would be natural that their planning would reflect French interests and desires, and thus have a political element to their goals. An operational report by the SAS clearly demonstrates their suspicions of and their contempt for the Alsatian Maquis.

"DO NOT DISSEMINATE

Capt.Druce is so definite in his opinion of the Maquis as he has observed them that he makes the following comments and recommendations.

The Maquis with few exceptions have shown a decided disinclination to undergo the hardships of guerrilla fighters and an unwillingness to engage the enemy. They have hidden and thrown away many weapons and on occasions have disappeared during combat.

Working with Lt.Colonel. Franks SAS unit is one Capt. Gough the surviving member of a 3 man Jedburgh Team. Capt.Druce states that Gough made a rather poor impression and was only awaiting an opportunity to make his way through to the American lines. Capt. Druce says that Capt.Gough upon contact with Allied forces will propose the following:

Gough and Col.Maximum (Fr) will request an air drop of 10 planes to supply arms to the Maquis. This drop will be proposed for approximately 10 hours prior to Allied arrival in Alsace. Druce states that this proposal is based on political motives, does not represent a "will to fight" and is for the purpose of "making an entrance" into Alsace in company with Allied troops. Druce states that Col.Maximum may have 10/15 Maquis who were originally porters and guides but later deserted the SAS. Those will be represented as the nucleus of the Gough/Maximum scheme. Druce believes that these men will almost literally "never fire a shot", that they cannot now muster any appreciable force, that their leadership will probably be weak and that their effort would in no way justify the expenditure of a 10 plane drop.

MAQUIS

General comments

1. They are disbanded, inoperative, or in hiding because of:

> *(a) Poor leadership*
> *(b) Faulty organisation*
> *(c) Lack of weapons*
> *(d) Informers within their ranks*

2. SAS camps and supply points were "tipped off" to the Germans, on six occasions in two months. This duplicity is believed to have been <u>within</u> the Maquis, as a result of:

> *(a) Fear*
> *(b) Rewards*
> *(c) Pro-German feeling*

3. the Maquis in this area, with few exceptions is considered:

> *(a) Unreliable*
> *(b) Unwilling to fight*
> *(c) Unwilling to undergo the hardships of Maquis life*
> *(d) Unlikely to be of any real assistance"*

If conditions were bad in early September they grew worse as autumn set in. It was wet and cold, producing poor conditions for re-supply airdrops. "Action Waldfest" had begun on September 1st and continued into October with increased German activity in the hills and a growing number of betrayals by locals to the Germans.

Jeeps brought in by air proved to be virtually useless and Colonel Franks had a lengthening list of defective weapons and equipment. With the weather conditions in October worsening and General Patton's advance stalled Brian Franks abandoned Operation Loyton and ordered his remaining men to make their way as best they could towards the Allied Front lines.

Throughout all this, Captain Gough of Jedburgh team "Jacob" operated independently of the SAS. He had been seen at the end of September by Lt. Col. Franks and Captain Sykes of 2 SAS. His SOE Battle Casualty report shows that he was known to have been with the Maquis de Reciproque during early October. It gives his time of capture only as "late October." A telegram sent by Col. Grandval (codename Planete) to SOE suggests that Gough was trying to make his way back to Allied lines near Senones. On February 9th 1945 Col. Grandval wrote to Lt. Col. Carleton-Smith (DR/JED) at SOE in Baker St, in part he said:

> *"A friend of mine, M. de Bouvier is without any news of his son Henry since middle of October.*
> *Henry de Bouvier was in a Maquis in the Vosges area, he was known in the underground as "Fred" and is supposed to have exfiltrated on or around 15th October with Captain V.A.Gough (Nr.148884 Somerset Light Infantry) of Jedburgh team JACOB.*
> *Presuming Captain Gough has safely come back, could he answer me or directly to M. Ch. de Bouvier………"*

Mrs. Baird also received an undated note from an officer of the FFI, in part he wrote:

> *"On September 4th we had fierce fighting with the Germans in the area of Badonviller, where Lt. B (Baraud) died as a hero. After that we had to break, Captain Gough came with us. More than a month we lived together in the woods, sleeping under parachutes. It was a very bad life. Soon Captain Gough decided to escape through the lines. We had lost all our wireless sets and had no more relations with London. I was determined to go with Captain Gough, but my French Colonel refused it. He sent one of my comrades, the nephew of the Lieutenant-Colonel and since we have had no news of them both, perhaps you have. In this case I would be very happy to know what happened to Captain Gough who was always a good man to all my boys.*
>
> *signed. A Vuillard"*

Sadly Captain Gough had not returned safely.

Gough was probably captured by Einsatz Kommando Ernst in late October, for he was seen at Maison Bartlemy in Salles which was the HQ of Kommando Ernst.

Following the August captures of Seymour, Hall, and Davis, Team "Loyton" continued to lose men.

19th September 1944:

Sgt. Fitzpatrick, Parachutist Elliot & Conway. Murdered at La Fosse Farm near Pexonne by Kommando Wenger, whose signature was also to burn the corpses. Witness Leon Muller saw the 3 men all in uniform, as prisoners, 2 in a car and 1 in a truck, going to La Fosse Farm. He heard bursts of machine gun fire and saw black smoke from a shed on fire. The owners of the farm M & Mme. Jacquet were also murdered.

21st September (about):

Lt.Black, Sgt Terry-Hall, Cpls.Iveson & Winder; Parachutists: Crozier, Dowling, Lloyd & Salter. Having taken refuge in a sawmill at La Turbine they were betrayed by their own Maquis guide Gaston Matthieu. After a four hour gun battle, having exhausted their ammunition they surrendered. They were captured on 15th September and seen briefly at Schirmeck Camp by the camp registrar Mlle. Joanne Hertenberger. Murdered at St.Die by Kommando Ernst.

5th October.

Parachutist J. Wertheim. Taken prisoner with Lt. Birnie and four other members of Team"Pistol". Held captive at the Rue de Fils Prison at Strasbourg. After interrogation the other five were sent to a normal POW Camp. Wertheim however was a German Jew by origin who had before the war left his homeland and joined the French Foreign Legion. He was sent to Niederbuhl Camp another of Karl Buck's satellite camps. He was murdered about 2nd December 1944. His Foreign Legion pay book was discovered at the camp after it was liberated.

15th October (about):

Sgts. Hay & Neville, L/cpls Robinson & Austin; Parachutists Bennett, Weaver, McGovan, & Church. This was Lt. Dill's group captured on 6th October and held for 2 days at Schirmeck camp, as seen by camp registrar Mlle. Hertenberger. Dill was later returned to the camp, for he was in the group murdered at Gaggenau. The rest were murdered at La Grand Fosse by Kommando Ernst

16th October.

Parachutists Brown & Lewis. Murdered in a farm building at La Harcholet by Kommando Wenger. Bodies burnt. A boxing medal belonging to Brown was found in the ashes

16th October.

Lt.Silly was a prisoner of Kommando Wenger, and seen by four members of the Lyautey family being taken into a shed with another British parachutist and a civilian at Maison Quiron at Le Harcholet. Lt. Silly was seen wearing a peaked cap and glasses. His corpse was burnt and he was identified by his spectacle case.

Date unknown.

Parachutist Puttick. Murdered by Kommando Wenger. Last seen in a Gestapo car laden with cans of petrol. There is strong evidence that Puttick was killed with Brown and Lewis on 16th October as a Middlesex Regiment badge was found in the ashes. Puttick had joined SAS from the Middlesex Regiment.

By early November the only SAS/Jedburgh parachutists still alive in the hands of the B.D.S. in the Vosges area (apart from Sgt.Seymour) were, Major Reynolds (wounded), Captain Whately-Smith, Lt. Dill, parachutists Griffin & Ashe, together with Captain Victor Gough team leader of "Jacob". Reynolds and Whately-Smith had been sheltered for some weeks by a retired couple Freddy and Miriam Le Rolland. Myriam Le Rolland had been a nurse in Paris for many years and was able to keep Reynold's wound free from gangrene. At the end of October a Mme. Le Blanc volunteered to guide them to the American lines something she had done previously for 3 other "Loyton" men. On this occasion it seems she led the two officers into a trap and they were captured by Wehrmacht troops at La Trouche.

Parachutist Ashe was not a member of Team "Loyton" but of SAS Team "Pistol" operating in the same general area. He was captured alone in a farm house which may have been the excuse for Schneider's men to classify him as a "terrorist". Of some ten officers and men from Team "Pistol" who were captured, only two, Ashe and Wertheim were murdered. The others were treated as normal POW's, in stark contrast to the "Loyton" men, none of whom survived captivity.

In the "post operations" report file on "Loyton" by 2 SAS (originally marked "Top Secret" not to be opened for 75 years) there is a single page memorandum by a Captain. C.D. Morgan who had been a POW from 1940 to 1944.The SAS it seems were trying to appreciate the difficulties their captured men might be enduring and they turned to Captain Morgan for a personal insight into what those men might expect. There is no indication with this document that Capt. Morgan had any psychological training; but this is what he wrote about encounters with the Gestapo.

> *"The Gestapo retains prisoners for interrogation. It is common practice for military prisoners captured in civilian clothes or for men captured under unusual circumstances (such as would the case with parachutists behind the lines) to be held by the Gestapo for varying periods of time. They are subjected to rigorous treatment in the hope of breaking down their morale or reticence. The methods usually adopted are close confinement, minimum rations, lengthy and fatiguing examinations, and denial of privileges such as correspondence, books, and Red Cross comforts.*
>
> *It is usual for prisoners held by the Gestapo to be transferred to normal Wehrmacht Camps, when the Gestapo feel satisfied that no more information is to be obtained from them.*
>
> *The men I saw who had been subjected to confinement by the Gestapo spoke of it as being an extremely trying and disagreeable experience. No cases of maltreatment implying physical violence were reported to me, or otherwise came to my notice"*

Sadly the captured Loyton officers and Jedburgh Captain Gough were subject to violence. Whatley-Smith and Gough were both taken to Maison Bartlemy at Salles where they were beaten. A witness Abbe Hett also saw Major Reynolds at Strasbourg strung up by his wrists and beaten until bone was visible through his flesh. Reynolds had also been assaulted at Maison Bartlemy his stomach having been stamped on repeatedly. This punishment was witnessed by Armand Souchais and Mme. Claudel. This appears to be the handiwork of "Stuka" the nickname of Wachtfuhrer Neuschwanger of Schirmeck Camp the said nickname acquired from his penchant for stomping on prostrate prisoners.

All the British captives were housed at the Sicherungs camp at Schirmeck a satellite of the notorious concentration camp at nearby Natzweiler. Whilst at Schirmeck Captain Gough produced a number of cartoon drawings which survived and were found by the SAS Investigation team. Several were reproduced in Major Barkworth's report "Missing Parachutists" in 1945. Schirmeck, often shown to neutral journalists as an example of a "musterlager," a humane and well organized camp, was situated outside the town in a valley leading to the Donon. Construction began in the summer of 1940 supervised by its permanent commandant Karl Buck. With a capacity of up 1500 prisoners it held both male and female inmates with 11 barracks for men and 3 for women. Karl Buck, who had worked abroad as a civil engineer, was an early member of the Nazi Party moving from the Stuttgart Gestapo in 1940 to take up his post at Schirmeck. As a result of wounds received in WW 1 Buck had a leg amputated in 1930 and during his time at Schirmeck was a regular user of morphine to combat both the pain in his stump and gangrene which was affecting his good leg. He suffered from mood swings and his temper was feared throughout the camp, more by staff than inmates. Until the summer of 1944 the prisoners at Schirmeck were mainly French, Alsatian, Russian, and Polish, that summer a few baled out airmen were brought to the camp before being sent by Buck for execution at Natzweiler.

In 1943 a large hall had been built at the western end of the camp mainly as a work place for women prisoners, but underneath the hall there was a complex known as the Steinbunker of 25 cells and a washroom with a further 6 cells near the washroom, intended primarily for women prisoners. It was in this basement area that the remaining six British parachutists were housed. They were to share their accommodation with 4 captured US airmen.

Lt. G.P.Jacoby of 388 Bomb Group baled out of his stricken bomber in the Donon region. He was captured around 5th September and brought to Schirmeck.

Sgt. Michael Pipock, a waist-gunner, was wounded in the thigh as he baled out over the Donon on September 10th.His wounds were treated secretly by a Dr.Stoll, a prisoner working in the camp hospital. (He also tended to SAS Major Reynolds who had been wounded prior to capture)

Sgts. Curtis Hodges and Maynard Latten baled out of their bomber on 5th September near Volksberg. They succeeded in evading capture until October 12th. They arrived at Schirmeck on October 17th, but their situation was unusual as they were captured almost 100 miles north of Alsace. Possibly the fact they were wearing civilian clothes over their uniforms and had been sheltered by French civilians was sufficient to classify them as terrorists and an excuse to send them to Schirmeck. Both men were in bad physical shape when captured.

In addition to the Americans, 4 Frenchmen were held in the cells 3 of them priests, Abbe Roth, Abbe Claude, Father Pennarath, and Werner Jakob an Alsatian.

On September 19th 1944 an unusual prisoner was added to the basement cell block, Untersturmfuhrer Werner Helfen of the Schutz Polizei. He had commanded a company guarding various official buildings. They were ordered back to the Vosges area on 16th August as the Allies advanced. Shortly after that date they were disarmed of their normal weapons and issued with sawn-off shotguns. On reaching Chalons-sur-Marne, Helfen ordered his men to throw their shotguns into the river. His reasoning was that such weapons were forbidden to soldiers under the Hague Convention, and if captured with them, they would lose their P.O.W. status. Helfen was arrested and on 26th August sentenced to death by an S.S.Court in Vittel for "willful destruction of Government property". In the "Block" Helfen was given the job of fetching and carrying food for the others, thus allowing him some freedom to move about the camp. Lager Wachmeister Joseph Muth in his sworn statement of 21st September 1945 remembers Helfen.

"There were 2 prisoners in the camp who, although confined in the cells, were given the task of bunkerwearter. One was a former Untersturmfuhrer and the other an Alsatian named Scherer. Scherer was used as a stool-pigeon. The other was German and behaved well towards his co-prisoners, For example I can remember that he had the French doctor brought to see to Pipock's wounds, although this was forbidden, and that he used to obtain extra food to supplement the very meager rations which the prisoners in the cells received"

Alongside the outer wall of the hall above their cells Helfen noticed there was a large silo for potatoes, constructed of numerous wooden slats. This gave him the idea of building a folding ladder with which to escape over the perimeter fence behind the hall. He broached the idea with Abbe Roth who spoke good English and German, and Captain Gough. The other prisoners were brought into the plan and work began at night, when patrols were less vigilant, utilizing stolen slats. Gough, Lt. Dill who had taught Helfen to play poker, and US officer Lt. Jacoby took turns in construction, covering themselves with blankets to deaden any noise. At the outset of their escape plan, the Allied advance deep into France was seen as an advantage, as fear and apprehension in their captors mounted. An Allied announcement that Camp Commandants would be held totally responsible for crimes committed in their camps also reached the prisoners ears, despite attempts to suppress the news by camp staff. Earlier in November Buck had wanted to send the parachutists to their deaths at Natzweiler Concentration camp, only to be told they were no longer admitting prisoners for execution.

Eventually the prisoners in the block settled on 12th November 1944 as the night for the escape. During the day of the 12th however Allied artillery fire became more intense than previously, for the first time they could also hear the sound of small arms fire., and the guess was that the front line was some 10 to 15 kilometres away. Wave upon wave of Allied aircraft swept overhead and the bomb blasts were louder and closer than before. Doubts began to surface, according to Werner Helfen, as the British captives weighed up the risks of escape against the chances of staying put and being rescued by the Allies. Abbe Roth and Helfen both tried to convince the others that the Nazis would not give up the camp without a struggle when the Allies arrived. Many of the 400 odd prisoners could lose their lives. Helfen recalled that all hope of escape was finally extinguished when it was announced that Schirmeck camp was to be evacuated, moving the prisoners further east to another camp at Gaggenau.

On November 17th Karl Buck, Commandant of Schirmeck Camp received a visit from B.D.S.Chief Eric Isselhorst. Buck's sworn statement of 22nd September 1945 recalls the encounter:

> *"When the situation became militarily acute and Schirmeck was threatened by the Allied advance I received secret orders from Dr.Isselhorst. He instructed that all inmates of the cells and such special persons as I might select were to be shot, the women prisoners were to be released and also to burn down the camp.*
>
> *These orders were not carried out at Schirmeck for the following reasons, first, I did not consider it wise to leave fresh mass graves behind, and secondly, I considered the camp might have been useful to the Wehrmacht who were retreating towards Schirmeck*
>
> *I drove to Gaggenau on 21st November and arranged with the Mercedes-Benz factory for a supply of sufficient trucks to evacuate the male prisoners from Schirmeck, across the Rhine to Gaggenau."*

During their last night together at Schirmeck, November 22nd, Captain Victor Gough presented Werner Helfen with Gough's own SOE silk escape map as a token of friendship and a gesture of gratitude for all that Helfen had done for his fellow prisoners in the block,. What the men in the block did not know, was, they were about to make their final journey.

On the night of the 21/22nd November a large convoy under Lt. Nussberger left Schirmeck for Gaggenau, and on the following night the last trucks carrying the 10 Allied prisoners and Werner Helfen amongst others, left and by 6 a.m. were driving through the deserted streets of Strasbourg. From an interview with Major Barkworth in September 1945, Karl Buck describes what happened next.

"The last convoy was under the supervision of Ostertag and Muth. On the way Ostertag allowed a German officer of the Schutz Polizei to escape in Strasbourg. This officer had previously been confined to the cells under sentence of death Personally, I was extremely glad to hear he had escaped. At the time of departure from Schirmeck I would gladly have left the English and American prisoners behind had I known that their interrogation was completed"

Werner Helfen remained at liberty, finding his way back to his home in Offenburg, until he was taken prisoner by the advancing Allies. Helfen would later make the acquaintance of Major Barkworth and discover that his death sentence had been commuted by the SS Courts to life with hard labour.

On the 18th of November 1945 Major Barkworth gave Werner Helfen a letter of commendation which read as follows:

"Herr Werner Helfen was prisoner in the Sicherungs camp at Schirmeck la Broque. He was placed in this camp after being sentenced to death for sabotage of the German war effort.

During the time he spent in the cells of Schirmeck camp, he did the best he could to better the conditions for the English and American prisoners of war who were confined there. Although had he been discovered he would have been severely punished. In smaller matters such as obtaining extra food, and giving these prisoners exercise, both of which were otherwise not allowed them, and also in the development of an escape plan, he showed his good intentions.

As Commanding Officer of the War Crimes Team which has the task of investigating the murder of those airmen and parachutists who were confined at Schirmeck, I have had sufficient opportunity to convince myself through the statements of witnesses, of Helfen's attitude during the time he was imprisoned."

Signed E.A.Barkworth Major, Comd. S.A.S. War Crimes Investigation Team

At the end of the war, as an anti-Nazi, Werner Helfen was able to return to his civilian job as a police officer, retiring at the equivalent rank of

Assistant Chief Constable. Nearly 50 years after Schirmeck, Werner Helfen would re-appear in this story.

The irony of the retreat from Schirmeck camp was that within hours of the last prisoners departure on the 23rd November the Americans had captured the town of Schirmeck, and less than 3 hours after the prisoners had passed through Strasbourg, where Helfen made his escape, the Americans had occupied the city. Two days prior to their departure a letter was posted in Mulhouse to Henry W Dunning of the American Red Cross in Paris which sadly he did not receive until 11th December.

> *"I am sending you a list of American and British Prisoners held by the Gestapo at the Concentration camp of Schirmeck-la-Broque in Alsace.*
> *I was able to talk with them personally several times and promised to advise their families.*
> *Lt.G.P.Jacoby ASN 0556376 (American)*
> *Sgt.Michael Pipock ASN 1617683 (American)*
> *Captain Whateley-Smith SAS 113612 (Anglais)*
> *Major. Denis Reynolds 2 me SAS Regt.130856 (Anglais)*
> *Captain Victor Gough 148884 Somerset Light Infantry attached to HQ Special Forces*
> *Lt. David Dill 2 me SAS 265704 (Anglais)*
>
> *These officers were living on 8 November 1944.*
>
> *I hope that the Red Cross can do something for these men and their families.*

The letter was signed *G. Stoll*. With such accurate detail (e.g. the serial numbers and units) this can only have been the same Dr.Stoll who had earlier been present in the camp hospital at Schirmeck and had treated Pipock and Major Reynolds.

The convoy with the parachutists and aircrew arrived at Gaggenau just about noon on the 23rd November. As there were no cells there to put them in, they were housed in Barrack 3 and were seen in the next 36 hours by numerous other camp prisoners who testified that they were alive until at least after midday on November 25th 1944. Commandant Karl Buck issued his instructions:

"After the transfer of prisoners and staff to Gaggenau, I visited Wuensch who was Lagerfuhrer at Gaggenau I told him that on the orders of Dr.Isselhorst, British and American prisoners and certain others were to be killed. I told him to destroy any evidence which might lead to the discovery of this crime and to take such precaution as would be normal, such as destruction of papers bearing their names, and any uniforms or any other aids of identification that might be on their bodies. Wuensch assured me that this would be carried out and he did not ask me whether this was right in view of the fact that the British and Americans were prisoners of war"

Lagerfuhrer Wuensch intended to place Lt Nussberger in charge of the execution squad, to carry out Dr. Isselhorst's orders, but on the morning of the 25th November he was not immediately to be found. Instead Wachtfuhrer Heinrich Neuschwanger was told to prepare a team for the executions. Shortly after noon Lager Wachmeister Joseph Muth entered Barrack 3 and read out a list of fourteen names. Outside a truck was being refuelled. Those detailed to accompany the prisoners on their final journey were, Neuschwanger, Ostertag and Ullrich who would perform the executions, Muth and Dinkel who would guard the prisoners and secure the road into the woods, three sergeants Niebel, Vetter and Korb who would provide security around the chosen bomb crater, a prisoner, Arnold, was to drive the truck and four Russian prisoners equipped with shovels completed the team.

A witness at the subsequent War Crimes Trial in Wuppertal was Erwin Martzolf from Strasbourg. He had been arrested by the Gestapo on July 6th 1944 and sent to Schirmeck before being transferred to Gaggenau in early September.

"Whilst at Gaggenau I became acquainted with the six British and four American prisoners. I used to speak to them in French and English. They told me that whilst at Schirmeck some had been beaten with sticks, but they did not say when.

On 25th November at about 1400 hours they received an order and I saw them lined up preparatory to them being taken away from the camp. I was sitting in Barrack 3 when the order was given. I asked Captain Gough where they were going and he said he thought they were going to a Stalag camp. I shook hands with all of them and heard Zimmermann say "No packages – leave your packages here". Then I realized that there was to be a killing because in the same moment I saw some Russians with shovels on the truck and I also saw Neuschwanger, Ullrich, Ostertag and Dinkel with machine pistols.

That afternoon it was general knowledge in the camp that the prisoners had been killed.

Oberwachtmeister Willing told us about a conversation he had with Zimmermann. Willing was responsible for writing out death certificates usually within twenty four hours of a death. One day a prisoner died and the certificate was not made out in the allotted time. Zimmermann reproached Willing for not having made it out. Willing answered by saying "Why Zimmermann at the time you killed those English and American prisoners you were in no hurry to make out death certificates"

With the help of another prisoner, George Hammerling who worked in the camp Records Office, Martzolf had devised a code system using numbers with which he noted down the names of the Allied victims together with their dates of birth and service numbers. On his release from Gaggenau in May 1945 he handed over this information to Captain Edmund Bishop of the French Liaison Group of B.A.O.R. in Strasbourg.

The truck left camp at about 2.30pm driving through Gaggenau, heading towards the Cemetery where they turned right onto a track leading into the Erlich Forest that would bring them close to the bomb crater, Neuschwanger, in his sworn statement said that Ullrich had already selected the execution site, Ostertag in his statement claimed it was Neuschwanger. All the guards carried pistols, Neuschwanger, Dinkel, Ullrich, and Ostertag also had Schmeissers. Neuschwanger in his statement (26th February 1946) describes what happened:

"The driver followed the directions given him by Ullrich. We turned right along the track for a distance of about 75 metres and then stopped. Ostertag asked me how many prisoners we should do at a time. I suggested three, so he gave the order for the first three to jump down. (Ostertag says the opposite was true)*The first three were civilians. I remember that as we were marching them down the track one of them took a photograph out of his pocket and looked at it. We turned into the wood for a distance of 20 to 30 metres until we came to the bomb crater. On a signal from Ostertag who was walking in the middle, we each fired at the prisoner in front of us.*

Moments before his death one of the French priests, Abbe Claude made a desperate dash for freedom. Neuschwanger's statement captures the moment:

"My pistol however had a stoppage and the prisoner in front of me ran away through the wood. After he had covered a distance of about 60 metres he was stopped by a shot from either Niebel or Korb, and killed as he lay wounded on the ground by another shot through the head. We then took most of the clothes off the bodies. The clothes were removed on the express orders of Wuensch in order to make the bodies unrecognizable.
We then went back to the truck and fetched another three prisoners, at a sign from Ostertag we each shot the respective prisoner in front of us, through the back of the head. We took the clothes off the bodies and threw them into the crater.

Months later Werner Helfen would be interviewed by Major Barkworth, from whom he learnt in detail the fate of his fellow prisoners. Helfen wrote this:

"So it happened, that of all people, Abbe Claude of whom I have the best memories – He was the quietest, god-loving and selfless person in the prison – would be hunted down by these monsters"

In all Joseph Muth estimated the whole enterprise took about half an hour, when it was over Muth went up to the bomb crater.

> *"When the firing was over I went up into the woods, and saw a big bomb crater in which the corpses were lying. These dead bodies were covered up with earth. I noticed about 50 meters away from the crater, a pile of clothes and shoes which had been taken off the bodies, to which Neuschwanger had set fire. Some of our group kept the best shoes for themselves"*

Virtually all the bodies were stripped of clothing, as Muth describes, however the killers became careless. Abbe Roth's body had not been completely stripped. When the bodies were eventually discovered by the SAS War Crimes investigators, Abbe Roth was found to be wearing a distinctive knitted sweater made for him by his sister-in -law, and smuggled into the Schirmeck cell block in early November. His decomposing body was later identified by this sweater. Neuschwanger's statement to Major Barkworth continued:

> *"I think that everyone in the police party took either some clothing or shoes back with them. I know that Ostertag had a ring and a gold pocket watch. I had a pair of black boots and Dinkel had a leather case with a zip fastener containing travel necessaries. Somebody told me that an identity disc was lying on the ground. I then noticed a metal disc on a chain; I took this and threw it away in the woods. I was influenced by the thought that this might help to make the bodies unidentifiable. It is not true that Ostertag's machine pistol developed a defect, for he was present at the shooting of each group.* (Ostertag swore that after the killing of the ninth victim, his weapon jammed and the remaining five prisoners were shot by Ullrich and Neuschwanger) *He was extremely hard on those under his orders and threatened us with being brought before an SS Court martial if we did not carry out his orders.*
>
> *I gained the impression that he had not carried out the shooting in the woods unwillingly.*
>
> *On the way back we said among ourselves, now they are giving us prisoners of war to shoot, and I said I considered it a rotten trick of Willing and Zimmerman to pass such people on to us to shoot when we would have to take the responsibility"*

There was never any chance that these murders could be kept secret. Rumours spread like wildfire among the 400 remaining prisoners at Gaggenau, helped in large measure by prisoner/driver Arnold who made the daily delivery of prisoner/workers to the nearby Mercedes-Benz truck factory, affording him a constant opportunity to gossip. Commandant Karl Buck saw to it that the three executioners Ostertag, Neuschwanger and Ullrich were promptly dispatched to the notorious Haslach Camp in the hope of keeping the lid on things, but within 18 months most of the Germans had been tracked down and charged with war crimes. In addition to this catalogue of murders, the Germans took reprisals against the French civilian population. In the nearby small town of Moussey they rounded up 256 men and took them away. At the end of the war 144 of those men did not return to their homes. On the last Sunday of September they and the murdered men of 2 SAS are remembered at a service in Moussey.

On May 13th 1945 the bodies from the bomb crater in the Erlich Forest were re-buried in Gaggenau town cemetery by the French authorities Lt. David Dill's mother visited her son's grave in Gaggenau cemetery but found the town an unattractive industrial wasteland much devastated by Allied bombing. Eventually the British victims would be reburied in the Commonwealth War Graves cemetery at Durnbach.

The evil men who carried out these atrocities had not reckoned on the resolve of Brian Franks C.O. of 2 SAS Regiment to obtain justice for his missing parachutists, and the dogged qualities of his Intelligence Officer, turned man hunter, Major Eric Barkworth.

MAJOR ERIC BARKWORTH

In 1944 Major Eric Alastair Barkworth was the Intelligence Officer of 2nd SAS Regiment. A slim man with a schoolmasterly appearance Barkworth was not someone to take no for an answer, he was described by his colleagues as "brilliant, ruthless and eccentric". His duties were to brief personnel going on operations and to de-brief them on their return.

During the late summer and autumn of 1944 2 SAS was engaged on two separate parachute operations, "Loyton" and "Pistol" in the Vosges area of eastern France. Operation "Pistol" was intended to disorganise, by sabotage, the German's rearward communications during their retreat. "Loyton" was planned to be complimentary to Maquis activity in the area. All personnel on these two operations were dressed in khaki battledress with regimental flashes on their shoulders.

From mid August until early November 1944, 31 members of SAS teams "Loyton" and "Pistol" and 2 members of Jedburgh team "Jacob" were taken prisoner from these missions. Just one of them would survive the war; the remaining 32 were posted as missing. On May 15th 1945 Major Barkworth received orders from his C.O. Lt.-Colonel Brian Franks to go to France and investigate the circumstances surrounding these missing men. Working with a small staff Major Barkworth quickly became a skilled and determined detective, criss-crossing Northern Europe in search of clues that would lead to the arrest of such Germans responsible for what were now certain to be 32 murders.

The investigation of War Crimes was becoming a major pre-occupation for the Allies, but the conduct of such enquiries was fragmented and parochial. From D-Day onwards every activity of the Allies was conducted under the banner of SHAEF including investigations of alleged violations of the 1929 Geneva Convention, but in early 1945 however, SHAEF announced that it was disbanding its Standing Court of Enquiry, and that in future war crime investigations would be devolved onto respective Army Groups. Investigating war crimes in North West Europe fell to the Judge Advocate General Branch of 21st Army Group HQ. Unfortunately not everyone was told of this new arrangement.

Major Barkworth had unwittingly trodden on someone's toes and at the end of July 1945 HQ 1st British Airborne Corps received a "ticking off" because of Barkworth's "freelance" activities.

> *".....30th July from JAG Branch (War Crimes Section)*
> *"On receiving Major Barkworth's report steps will certainly be taken to investigate the cases referred to, and a British investigation team will be detailed.*
> *I must point out that none of these cases have yet been reported to 21 Army Group, nor have any copies of the SHAEF Courts of Enquiry been forwarded to this Department.*
> *Had Major Barkworth reported to this HQ, every assistance would have been given to him in his work, as reciprocal arrangements have already been made in the areas controlled by other nationalities and there are French Liaison authorities specially appointed at this HQ to deal with War Crimes".........*
> *Signed by Colonel Backhouse- Legal Staff*

In truth the Commander of 1st Airborne Corps had irritated JAG Branch of 21 Army Group by passing on to them some of Barkworth's criticisms of the shambles he found.

> *"...The confidential letter attached shows the difficulties which Major Barkworth has had to contend with through there being no British Crime Team in the area and through apparent lack of system and co-operation by French authorities. In this connection, it is reported that Weber, one of the main criminals, was traced by Major Barkworth to be living in comfort with a pass signed by a junior French officer stating that he, Weber, was a "harmless German"....*
> *26th July 1945 signed by I.G.Collins Lt.-Colonel Commander 1st Airborne*

On July 23rd 1945 Barkworth's own CO Brian Franks had written to Brigadier Calvert, Commander of SAS Regiments about the problems with the French. The following extract illustrates the difficulties.

"...Barkworth is working under extreme difficulty mainly due to the disorganization of the French. There are six different bureaux dealing with war crimes, it seems there is no co-ordinated head to these departments and complete lack of co-operation between them
The following are a few examples:
1) Information was received from a member of the staff at Schirmeck Camp that the card index file showing names of all prisoners who had passed through the camp, had been handed over to a Captain Martin 1st French Army. Barkworth interviewed this officer and after a wild chase round many Departments was told that as the index only concerned American and British personnel it was of no interest to the French and had been destroyed.
2) 5 bodies found by the French at a camp near Baden-Baden were removed and now no French authorities appear to know where they are.
3) A man held by the French for black market activities turned out to be the official Gestapo photographer at Strasbourg. When Barkworth interviewed him he had photographs of one of the missing SAS officers and of a Jedburgh wireless set. He had never been searched by the French

At the end of this confidential memo Franks wrote.

.... I am sure you will understand my feelings in this matter. At present I very much doubt whether even a small percentage of the perpetrators of these crimes will be brought to justice. I feel personally responsible, not only to the families of these officers and men but also to the men themselves. There are no lengths to which I would not go to ensure that action is taken"....

On the same day, 23rd July, Lt.Col. Franks wrote a highly critical letter to Major Barry Thomas at Special Forces in Baker St.

"As promised on the telephone, I enclose copy of Major Barkworth's report since it contains a good deal of information regarding the fate of Captain V.Gough who was with me in the Vosges, and whose death is now proved.

It is very surprising to me that Special Force have never taken the trouble to make any enquiries whatever regarding this officer's fate. Unfortunately I do not know the address of his next of kin and, therefore am unable to write to them. No doubt Special Force will do so."

(In fact on September 18th 1945 Lt.Colonel Brian Franks did send a letter of condolence via SFHQ to Gough's next of kin).

Within a week Brigadier Calvert was trying to pull strings by calling in a favour from an old friend Lt.Colonel Martin Lindsay, Member of Parliament. On the 31st July Calvert wrote to Lindsay at the House of Commons, in part this is what he wrote.

"First British Airborne Corps are taking the matter up officially, but the difficulty at the moment is due to the disbandment of so many HQ, and it is difficult to find any one HQ which is fully responsible for this subject. This is accentuated by the fact that most HQ now have an end of term feeling and are reluctant to take on extra and rather complicated subjects.
Also the fact that the British are not by nature a revengeful race makes it more difficult to convince people that this is not a matter for revenge but of bringing criminals to justice.
The main snag is there is no one authority who can deal with all these charges, as there seems to be little co-operation between Americans, French and British.
I feel that if you could mention the matter to the Under Secretary of State for War and ask him to look in to it, it would have immediate results in there being more interest taken in the matter. I do not want this done in order that someone might be rapped over the knuckles, but purely to obtain results.
I should be glad if you could avoid mentioning the source of information."…..

With this letter Calvert enclosed both Barkworth's Interim Report and a copy of Lt.Colonel Frank's confidential memo. (Lt.Colonel Lindsay would remain a good parliamentary friend to the SAS. Hansard reports that on 28th January 1947 he was still pressing Secretary of War Bellinger for progress reports on the trials of the 2 SAS murderers. Secretary Bellinger reported that in the cases of Lt.Silly, Sgt.Fitzpatrick, troopers

Elliot, Conway, Lewis, and Brown investigations were underway, but that trials were yet to take place.)

On the 3rd of August 1945 Lt.-Col. I.G.Collins Commander 1st Airborne Corps wrote a placatory note to JAG Branch 21 Army Group HQ in the hope of soothing ruffled feathers, in part he wrote:

"It is much regretted that the wrong channel of approach has been used. The SAS operations concerned were, however, carried out in 1944 under SHAEF command in an American area and all previous correspondence has been conducted through SHAEF and the War Office and we were never informed that 21 Army Group would be entirely responsible for the investigations......"

On August 8th Colonel Backhouse of JAG Branch 21st Army Group replied to Lt.Colonel Collins and from the tenor of his letter the ruffled feathers were now soothed:

1) Major Barkworth 2 SAS has now reported to me and has given full details of his investigations, and I have arranged for No.1 War Crimes Investigation Team to proceed to Gaggenau, where Major Barkworth has returned, with a view to making a full investigation in respect of the SAS personnel concerned in that area.
2) You will appreciate that my letter of 30th July was not intended to raise any criticism but merely to ensure that from now on cases might be investigated as quickly as possible and that you might be aware of what assistance could be placed at your disposal"

On the 10th August Commander 1st Airborne wrote to Major Barkworth hoping to put his mind at rest over the shortcomings of the system.

"Subject: War Crimes

1. I congratulate you on the result of your work and on your very fine report. I can assure you that we are doing all possible here to help you and to ensure that these SAS cases are brought to the attention of the correct authorities.

2.You have, in one or two signals, queried our efforts but it would be a waste of time to go back over past history and there is no doubt the High Command authorities were slow in getting down to this War Crimes policy and in getting an organisation to work smoothly.

You queried why we did not put you in touch with 21 Army Group in the first place and why they did not get a copy of your report. The answer is that if 21 Army Group were going to handle these cases SHAEF should have told you when you saw them on 9th June. War Office did not know until a week or ten days ago that 21 Group would handle cases outside their area of occupation and there has undoubtedly been a lack of liaison between WO and 21 Army Group which meetings this week have, I think, put on a more correct basis. I received today a letter dated 8th August from Colonel Backhouse JAG Branch which was very friendly and he has indicated that he will give all possible support to these cases.......”

With that note Lt.Colonel Collins enclosed a diagram laying out the lines of responsibility that were to be followed. The diagram's footnote explains:

…War Crimes Teams will send all their cases through 21 Army Group to JAG Branch who decide after reading evidence whether the case should be proceeded with and against whom, and then arrange for a Court to try the accused personnel <u>with a view</u> to getting them condemned and shot or hung”…..

Major Barkworth underlined the words in the last sentence and underneath it made this observation in pencil. *“An interesting précis of the principles of British Justice!!”*

The following week Lt.Colonel Collins 1st Airborne Corps wrote to the Under Secretary of State at the War Office seeking to explain why Barkworth had embarked on his investigations, and again highlighting complaints against the French:

The arrangements for Major Barkworth's investigations in the Vosges etc were made last spring with Colonel Page, G-1 SHAEF, who up until June 1945 handled all our correspondence in this matter. We are closing down in a week or two and I am afraid we have already destroyed the file containing Colonel Page's letter authorizing the investigations.

2 SAS on whose strength Barkworth is held as I.O. may also be disbanded shortly. It is noted that you may be able to arrange for Barkworth to be absorbed into your organisation to continue his work."

Lt.Colonel Collins was highly critical of the French Security system.

"Incompetence of French Authorities

This is instanced by the following:

a) The general attitude of the French is that victims are martyrs and Germans are brutes. Faced with these woods they are unable to see the trees which compose them and do not make detailed intelligent investigations as to the identity of the victims or the responsibility of criminals.

b) There 6 different French departments all more or less bearing on the war crimes. There appears to be absolutely no liaison between them and a certain jealousy prevents them from pooling information.

Finally the French War Crimes authorities fail to tie up adequately with the British and American organisations. This may be perhaps due to the fact that the French War Crime Teams were turned out of American occupied Germany as the Americans said they did nothing but loot.

Dishonesty of the French

It is regrettable that not only have we encountered an inexpert attitude of mind, but also very evident double dealing both towards us and towards the principle of suppressing former Nazi elements.

The Surete Nationale have working for them at Strasbourg an Alsatian, named Uhring, who was formerly with the Gestapo at Strasbourg where it appears he interrogated British prisoners of war. It is believed that the majority of missing SAS personnel were interrogated by the Gestapo there, and this mans evidence would be invaluable to us to prove exactly who did go to Strasbourg. Unfortunately we are not allowed to see him as he is alleged to be writing his memoirs and must not be disturbed."...

Marie Alphonse Uhring was indeed a key figure as part of the Strasbourg triumvirate of Schneider, Gehrum and Uhring who instigated *"Action Waldfest"* and between them were responsible for the murders of British parachutists in the Vosges.

Lt.Col.Collins cited another instance which can only be described as a "French Farce"

"On 15th June Major Barkworth called on O.R.C.G.(the French team hunting war criminals) *at Baden-Baden giving them a list of wanted men, asking them to let him know if any were picked up and to send copies of the list to their branches at Lindau and Strasbourg. Three weeks later Barkworth visited Lindau O.R.C.G. and found they had not received his wanted list. He left a copy there. Towards the end of July he visited Paris with Captain Sykes and was informed by Commandant Beckhart 2nd i/c O.R.C.G. that Ostertag one of the wanted men, had been taken prisoner 3 miles from Gaggenau and would be in Paris in a week or ten days, and meanwhile was being held at Baden-Baden. On returning to the area he called on O.R.C.G. at Baden-Baden with a request to interview Ostertag. They denied any knowledge of Ostertag and he was invited back for lunch in five days by which time something might have turned up. He kept the date but found his host had left for Paris. He called back two days later to remind them that Commandant Beckhart had said Ostertag had been taken near Gaggenau. They denied any knowledge of Ostertag. At that moment Commandant Beckhart entered and Barkworth said "Where is Ostertag?" Beckhart said "Oh, he was here but he's gone to Paris now", and turned to the other officer for confirmation which was promptly forthcoming, thereby giving the lie to his own remarks of a minute previous. Two days later Barkworth went to Paris and called on O.R.C.G. and met Commandant Beckhart in a corridor and exchanged words before going in to see the head of the Paris O.R.C.G. Colonel Montout. He denied all knowledge of Ostertag and, unaware Barkworth had just spoken with Beckhart in the corridor outside, made a pretence of trying to ring up Commandant Beckhart in Baden-Baden, finally telling Barkworth, the lines were down!.(Shortly afterwards, in another office, a telephone call to Baden-Baden on another matter was successfully made) From the foregoing it appears perfectly clear*

that the O.R.C.G. is in some way interested in denying us access to these vital witnesses whom it seems indubitable that they hold".

By now 21st Army Group had established their own No.1 War Crimes Investigation Team but Major Barkworth's "free-lance" activities were still causing some irritation.

On September 24th 1945 Lt-Colonel Leo Genn O/C No 1 War Crimes Team wrote to Lt-Col Harris at H.Q. B.A.O.R. At this time 18 SAS men were still missing, presumed murdered. In part he wrote:

"In the case of the 18, despite strenuous efforts by Barkworth and his team and at least a fortnight's work by officers of this team, no clue which could provide results has been found. Purely as a matter of opinion, I am convinced that only a miracle will now provide such a clue.

The situation is that Barkworth is continuing to search, but it is obviously not part of this Team's duty to seek for clues to establish crimes, but to endeavour to establish and prove a crime when some initial clue has been given. In other words, our objective begins where the SAS objective ends and that is the reason why we have returned from the area in the belief that there is little further useful work we can do.

Just for your own information, I feel I ought to point out that there is one other difference between SAS investigation and ours. This is that although the SAS are in many ways extremely valuable as investigators, Barkworth's material conforms to no known legal standard of proof and is very often based on pure hearsay, neither is it ever, to the best of my belief, reduced to writing, and that a considerable proportion of what he gets could not possibly be used for our purposes without going over the ground again and using our own established means as laid down by JAG and yourselves"

Lt-Colonel Harris then wrote to his counterpart at the War Office in London in a confidential memo of October 6th 1945. Apart from repeating what Lt-Col. Genn had told him, Harris added the following criticism of Major Barkworth.

"Barkworth and his party have made themselves somewhat unpopular with the French, who feel considerable resentment at the way they have circulated in

French territory without apparently informing the French of their presence and intentions, and have finally written a report on the attitude of the French which the French regard as highly offensive. He has now applied to USFET for a laissez passer for his party in the American Zone; the Americans have referred the matter to us but before we back the application we would like to have him and his team officially attached to this HQ. We can then brief him as to the need for tact in Allied Zones before we let him loose.

We would like this attachment to be for the purposes of war crimes investigation in general, and NOT exclusively for the SAS case."

Lt-Colonel Genn still had plenty to say about Major Barkworth and his methods, when he wrote on 9th November 1945 to JAG Branch at B.A.O.R.

"In my opinion there is nothing further to be got from investigating, other than a light on perpetrators or the apprehension thereof. In this connection I feel I can honestly say that I do not understand how Barkworth has arrested 70 perpetrators, as I do not believe that anything like that number are involved; and also, that a very great deal of what the so-called SAS Team were doing, and as I understand it is still doing, is misguided and of no value; except of course insofar as they may do the police work, which we do not deal with, and arrest or trace perpetrators".

However despite the complaints and the "local difficulties" with the French, Barkworth was making progress. His investigation into the Gaggenau murders had discovered that besides the SAS and Special Forces victims there were 4 French civilians (including possibly 3 priests) and 4 US airmen buried all together in a bomb crater. In September 1945 an appeal on radio and in the local press in Strasbourg, was made for witnesses to the murders to come forward. On occasions his team would need to rely on subterfuge to catch up with wanted men. In a 1970's TV documentary "The Secret Hunters" Captain Prince Yurka Galitzine of Barkworth's team recalled how they had tracked down Lt. Neuschwanger (one of the Gaggenau killers) only to discover he was hiding in the Russian controlled Zone, beyond official British jurisdiction. A telephone call to Neuschwanger offering him a juicy stake in a bogus blackmarket fraud was sufficient to lure him into the British Zone and captivity. In the same TV documentary, Warrant Officer "Dusty" Rhodes, one of Barkworth's team recalled how they took Neuschwanger back to the bomb crater site in the Erlich Forest. On being asked if he had any remorse for his crimes Neuschwanger reacted with coldness and distain, whereupon W/O Rhodes lost his temper and punched Neuschwanger, sending him crashing into the bomb crater with a foot of rainwater at the bottom. W/O Rhodes then remarked *"He was fortunate because he was coming out of it again, unlike the men he had put in there"*.

Finding suitable witnesses also presented problems for the SAS team, as Major Barkworth noted in his "Missing Parachutists" report:

"It has been a matter of some difficulty to trace and select reliable witnesses to account accurately for the presence at Schirmeck of the British and American prisoners confined there.

After the beginning of September 1944 a register was kept of such POWs, but before that date no records which were kept, have been found,

The statements of many prisoners in the camp are of extremely doubtful value for the following reasons:

(a) Prisoners confined in such a camp for a long period, have in general no memory for dates.

(b) They are often confused and cannot differentiate between airmen, parachutists and other types.

(c) Many of these statements are based on hearsay camp gossip, and therefore it is easy enough to understand that the prisoners in Schirmeck, below the hill on which stood Natzweiler camp, should assume that every truck leaving the former should be bound for the "execution" camp.

(d) Certain prisoners wish to increase their own importance and status as political martyrs by making definite statements concerning cases of which they have no personal experience or knowledge.

Brian Franks C.O. of 2 SAS had assumed a more optimistic outlook when he wrote again to Brigadier Calvert:

"On the brighter side, there is an American War Crimes Team headed by Col. Chavez assigned to investigate crimes against American aircrew at Gaggenau. This team includes 2 pathologists, a professional interpreter, 2 lawyers, shorthand typists and photographers. It is clearly a highly efficient organisation. Barkworth has worked in close co-operation with them and they have exceeded their duty in investigating the cases of this regiment. I had a long talk with Col.Chavez and was much impressed by his desire to help us. He expressed amazement that the British investigation of 27 cases should be left in the hands of a single officer...."

By the end of December 1945, just 6 months since the Barkworth team had started their investigations, evidence gathered from interrogations showed the Germans to have been enforcing a rigorous policy towards Allied parachutists. Still at an early stage in their searches and with many Germans still to be interrogated, Captain Sykes 2 SAS (formerly of team" Loyton") part of the Barkworth team, wrote an assessment of what they believed that policy to be.

"It seems clear from the findings of the Loyton post-operational investigations that a definite policy lies behind German treatment of paratroops. None of the atrocities discovered indicate murders committed in the heat of combat. As evidence of what policy directs these murders I am authorised by Madame Gerard of Le Harcholet to record that when she asked a German OR what would become of the prisoners lodged in her timber shed, he replied "They will be shot". She added "Surely not, since they are in uniform?" He answered "That makes no difference"
I am authorised by Doctor Wojnarowski of Senones to record that when he asked a Spezial Dienst officer Max Kessler what was done with paratroop prisoners, he replied "Paratroops captured in battle are treated normally, but Nachtschirmfalljager dropped behind the lines in small parties are shot as spies and saboteurs" When the Doctor asked for an explanation Kessler replied They do the same to our paratroops"
The better treatment accorded to the Team Pistol parties (according to present information) suggests that though there is an order enabling German commanders to shoot all paratroops of the SAS type, this is not always acted upon. It is noteworthy that all evidence so far concerning SAS prisoners of

War in both operations, mentions Gestapo guards. This indicates that all SAS prisoners remain in permanent Gestapo custody"

There was indeed a "definite" policy in place, issued by Hitler's Headquarters; known as "Order of 18 October 1942" After the D day landings a supplement to that order was also issued. A copy of these orders appears to have been recovered from an unknown German Command Headquarters captured some time after D-Day. The accompanying Allied memo, together with a translation of the orders in English, reads thus:

> *SECRET Report No. FF-2175*
> *German Orders to kill Captured Allied Commandos and Parachutists*
> *"The first of the following two orders was issued by the Fuehrer Headquarters on 18th October 1942 and re-issued, together with the supplementary order, on a date not indicated following the invasion of France. The German classification of the orders is "Most Secret". A covering note found with the two orders, dated 10th October 1944 indicates that the order was distributed to regimental commanders and staff officers of corresponding rank."*

Clearly these papers were captured some time after 10th October 1944. There is no indication of either the sender or recipients of this document once it fell into Allied hands. There were 6 paragraphs to the original order. The following extracts give a clear indication of intentions.

> *"1. Recently our adversaries have employed methods of warfare contrary to the provisions of the Geneva Convention. The attitude of the so-called commandos, who are recruited in part among common criminals released from prison, is particularly brutal and underhanded. We have captured orders which advocate putting prisoners to death as a matter of principle".*
> *"2. In future Germany will resort to the same methods in regard to these groups of British saboteurs and their accomplices – that is to say that German troops will exterminate them without mercy wherever they find them"*
> *"3.Therefore I command that henceforth all enemy troops encountered during so-called commando operations, though they appear to be soldiers in uniform,*

armed or unarmed, are to be exterminated to the last man. If such men appear to be about to surrender, no quarter should be given to them"

"4. If members of such units, acting as agents, saboteurs, etc., falls into the hands of the Wehrmacht they are to be handed over to the Sicherheitedienst without delay. It is formally forbidden to keep them, even temporarily, under military supervision (for example in Prisoner of War camps)

"5. These provisions do not apply to enemy soldiers who surrender or are captured in actual combat within the limits of normal combat activities. Nor do they apply to aviators who have baled out to save their lives during aerial combat".

"6. All leaders and officers who fail to carry out these instructions – either by failure to inform their men, or by their disobedience of this order, will be summoned before a tribunal of war."

The supplement issued after June 1944 was also quite clear:

1. "In spite of the Anglo-American landing in France, the Fuehrer's order of 18 October 1942 regarding the destruction of saboteurs and terrorists remains fully valid.

2. All members of terrorist and saboteur bands, including (on general principle) all parachutists encountered outside the immediate combat zone are to be executed. In special cases they are to be turned over to the SD"

3. All units outside the Normandy combat zone are to be given precise and succinct instructions on the duty incumbent upon them to destroy groups of terrorists and saboteurs."

I have underlined several sentences to highlight the main points as they impinged on the men of team "Loyton" and Jed team "Jacob". For example it is perfectly clear that the US Airmen at Gaggenau should never have been treated in the same way as the Special Forces prisoners. The words of the supplement make clear the attitude to parachutists, and suggest that Sgt. Seymour was made a "special case", following Schneider's claim, "Seymour had talked."

Early signs of the German attitude to parachutists were clearly visible on the ground immediately after D-Day. An American member of

Jed Team "Frederick" who were dropped into Brittany with an SAS Team in operation "Samwest" on 9th June 1944 later wrote:

> *"The Jed teams, like the SAS, were to drop in uniform so that we could more easily identify ourselves to the Resistance as legitimate representatives of Allied Headquarters. I do not recall any discussions of what to do in the event of capture. Some Jed teams were told that they could expect to be treated as POW's, if captured. Any illusion we may have had on this account was destroyed when, after arrival in France, we saw notices on buildings and along roads stating that parachutists were spies and would be treated as such"*

For Schirmeck Commandant Karl Buck, disobeying these instructions was out of the question. In his sworn statement to Major Barkworth of 22nd September 1945 he said:

> *"I stood in fear of Dr. Isselhorst, who I know would not only have me executed, but also would attack my family should I act contrary to his orders."*

On the 6th February 1946 Brigadier Shapcott of the Judge Advocate General's department was able to write to the C-in-C of B.A.O.R. to confirm that the Vosges killings were to be treated as a War Crime and a list of accused was drawn up. Major Barkworth's work would become crucial to these prosecutions. The accused however were scattered across Europe, some in custody with B.A.O.R., some with the French, and some with the US Army. A number of the lower ranked accused would also be required as witnesses in the trials of senior Nazis so it was agreed to postpone their committals until they had given evidence.

In the case of the Gaggenau killings matters were further complicated because the victims, in addition to British Special Forces, included 4 US Aircrew and 4 Frenchmen. Thus once the British had finished trying their accused, the French and Americans would be eager to bring their own charges against the same men. Eventually a number of accused would receive multiple death sentences imposed by the three separate judicial systems.

It had been agreed between the three prosecuting Nations that whichever Court handed down the most severe sentence the accused would be returned to that particular court for the sentence to be carried out. Some of the accused were still at liberty and so that they would not be forewarned that they were wanted on capital charges all publicity about the case was strictly forbidden. Sensitive to the mixed nationalities of the victims in the Gaggenau killings, JAG Branch invited the French and American authorities to provide up to 50% of the court panel trying the cases.

The first trial for the SAS murders was held in Wuppertal between 6th and 10th May 1946. Those on trial were essentially those who pulled the triggers at Gaggenau; those who gave the orders would follow. In this trial, apart from the pointing of fingers and passing of blame, the question of obeying orders was raised. Erwin Ostertag was asked this question:

> *Q. Do you know that shooting without trial and without judgement is equivalent to murder?*
> *A. There should be no foundation in the punishable accusation of intentional murder as the order for the execution of the action was given by official order. I know that generally speaking shootings only appear as the final conclusion of a court. I must, however, assume that the official order of my superior was correct"*

Defence Counsel claimed that there was evidence that the victims of the shootings had established such contact with "Terrorists" (i.e. the Maquis) as would bring them within the scope of the "18th October 1942" orders, and that a "security police case" preceded the executions. The accused would themselves have been punished by the S.S. had they not carried out their orders regarding the prisoners. Counsel for various individual accused claimed that the punishment meted out would undoubtedly have been death.

It is a rule of English law that ignorance of the law is no excuse: Ignorantia juris neminem excusat. There are some indications that this principle when applied to the provisions of international law is not regarded universally as being in all cases strictly enforceable. In the present trial, the Judge Advocate, in his summing up, said that the Court must ask itself: "What did each of these accused know about the rights of a prisoner of war? That is a matter of fact upon which the Court has to make up its mind. The Court may well think that these men are not lawyers: they may not have heard either of the Hague Convention or the Geneva Convention; they may not have seen any book of military law upon the subject; but the Court has to consider whether men who are serving either as soldiers or in proximity to soldiers know as a matter of the general facts of military life whether a prisoner of war has certain rights and whether one of those rights is not, when captured, to security for his person. *It is a question of fact for you.*"

Counsel acting for the accused in general pointed out that in Germany there had been not only courts-martial but also " so-called S.S. and police courts for German persons and members of the S.S." He claimed that the interrogations of the victims by Kommando fuhrer Ernst, on whose reports Dr. Isselhorst acted, constituted a trial by the Security Police. The accused he claimed had had no other information on the matter than that the prisoners had been tried and condemned, and had acted on that assumption. The accused had "neither the grasp of technicalities nor the mental abilities to look deeper into this case." The Prosecutor, on the other hand, submitted that the obliteration of all traces of the crime and the steps taken by the accused to suppress all knowledge of the crime belied any contention that they thought that they were performing a legal execution. Lawful executions did not take place in woods, nor were those shot buried in bomb craters with their valuables, clothing and identity markings removed.

The sentences passed were as follows: Death by shooting on Buck, Nussberger, Ostertag, Ullrich, and Neuschwanger, imprisonment for Zimmermann 10years, Dinkel 8 years, Wuensch 4 years, Korb 3years, Vetter 2years, acquitted Muth. All sentences subject to confirmation.

Dr. Eric Isselhorst head of the BDS Alsace was much in demand. Ten days before he was due to stand trial for his part in the Vosges murders JAG Branch received the following memo from the French War Crimes Mission.

> *"Subject: War Criminal ISSELHORST*
> *The above mentioned who is interned in C.I.C. No.4 is wanted by France as*
> *a war criminal for murders, slaughters, tortures and atrocities at Strasbourg*
> *where he was chief of the Gestapo, and a warrant of arrest has been issued by*
> *the Juge d'Instruction militaire of Strasbourg. Could this man be handed over*
> *to the French authorities?*

On the eve of the second Vosges trial a curious incident occurred. At 10.45pm Major Barkworth received a phonecall from a journalist called Main who worked for Reuters News Agency and was covering the trial. He disclosed to Barkworth, that he had a copy of Barkworth's "Missing Parachutists" report (known as the "Red Book" on account of the colour of its cover) and was intending to use some of the material in his reportage. Barkworth informed Major Hunt, Chief Prosecutor on the morning of the trial, and he wrote the same day to the Judge Advocate General's office in London. A subsequent investigation revealed that Main had "borrowed" this copy of the report from a British Officer involved with the War Crimes investigations. On the 11th July 1946 the War Office concluded that no law had been broken, since the Barkworth report although marked "confidential" had not been classified with any security grading. It was also known that an ex-SAS officer now working as a journalist had kept his copy, after leaving the Army, a copy he had been entitled to have during his service.

On 17th June 1946 the second trial began at Wuppertal (it was at this trial that Sgt.Seymour would appear as a defence witness for Schneider.) Here the scope broadened to cover the murders of other SAS in the Vosges region prior to the Gaggenau killings; hence Seeger, Oberg and Schlierbach of BDS France were in the dock together with Isselhorst, Schneider and Gehrum of BDS Alsace.
In Gehrum's trial he was cross examined by defence counsel Dr. Von Bruck representing a co-defendant on the question of obeying orders:

"Q. Have you ever heard of an order in the following words; "Every superior has the right, if a subordinate does refuse an order, to shoot him on the spot"?

A. I have heard about this order, but I do not know whether it was from the Fuhrer himself or from the Reich Fuhrer of the S.S. Himmler, and it came out as I remember in the middle of 1943. When the order came out it was shown to every man in the S.D., the Security Service, and he had to sign his name on it, that he had understood the wording; then every three months the same procedure was gone through again – every man had to sign his name that he understood the wording, and the order was put in his file"

The Judge Advocate stated that in principle superior orders provided no defence to a criminal charge, and made reference to that passage from Oppenheim-Lauterpacht's *International Law*, 6th Edition revised, pp. 452-453, on which reliance has been placed so frequently in war crime trials: He expressed the view that an accused would be guilty if he committed a war crime in pursuance of an order, first if the order was *obviously unlawful*, secondly if the accused *knew that the order was unlawful*, or thirdly if he *ought to have known it to be unlawful had he considered the circumstances in which it was given*.

The Judge Advocate pointed out that under The Hague Convention even spies were entitled to a trial. (Footnote: Article 30 of the Hague Convention No. IV of 1907: "A spy taken in the act shall not be punished without previous trial.") There seemed to him to be no evidence that the victims were ever tried before a Court. Dr. Isselhorst had said that they were sentenced by decision of Ernst and "not through a court." If his evidence was believed, they were condemned as a result of an administrative decision and not after a trial.

The case of General Willi Seeger was slightly different. Seeger was Commanding Officer of Wehrmacht Reserve Division No. 405 based at Strasbourg. This division was a rag bag of new young raw recruits, plus wounded men, now recuperating and released from hospital. It was claimed on his behalf that as CO of a Reserve Division, he was not on the circulation list of the "Hitler Order of October 1942" and therefore he was unaware of the "to kill" policy against parachutists.

Seeger claims he was told that Seymour had given valuable information away, but had no knowledge that Hall and Davis had been murdered in mid August 1944.

Brigadier Lord Russell of Liverpool writing on behalf of JAG to BAOR HQ summed it up as follows:

> *"The case of General Seeger is different from that of the other accused. He was not part of "Action Waldfest" organization and he could only be said to be concerned in the killing of the persons mentioned in the charge, in the sense that he had a duty and the power to prevent these soldiers being dealt with in a way he must have known would inevitably lead to their deaths"*

On 11th July sentences were pronounced, death by hanging, on Oberg, Isselhorst and Schneider, 10 years in prison for Schlierbach, 3years for Seeger, whilst Gehrum was acquitted. Gehrum's defence was based on strenuously refuting mainly allegations, suppositions, and pure gossip emanating from Gestapo colleagues. For example the mere fact of having been seen at Schirmeck camp at all, was perceived to mean that he was actively involved with the SAS prisoners, notwithstanding he could neither read nor speak English. His counsel Dr.Kohrs successfully demolished this hearsay evidence and secured his acquittal. At one stage in his lengthy summing-up Dr. Kohrs painted a chilling picture of what a secretive and fearful world the Third Reich had become.

> *"If the conduct of the SS and the Gestapo as a whole was such that it was wide open to suppositions, you must not be surprised at that. You already know what role the "Secret Reich" activities have played. In the course of this trial you have also heard of the Fuhrer order that immediately upon the start of the war was published and posted in every company's office, in every staff quarters, and in every officer's mess. According to this, no soldier, no officer either, was permitted to receive knowledge of things that did not have to be made known to him for official reasons.*
> *This duty to keep secret even unimportant matters was one of the causes why National Socialism was successful in suppressing the majority of the people for such a long time.*
> *It was dangerous to know too much. It was more dangerous to ask too much.*

It was still more dangerous to say too much.
The inevitable consequence, however was that the society in which supposition and rumours developed, was richly cultivated"

On the 4th of August 1946 Gehrum was extradited to the French to stand trial for a series of murders of French nationals. Unfortunately for Gehrum he had condemned himself in his own words in a statement of 22nd November 1945 to Major Barkworth

"After the evacuation of Strasbourg I was entrusted with the liquidation of certain prisoners, of whom a list was given me, first in Kohl on 23rd November, on the 24th November in Rastatt, on the 27th November in Offenburg and the 28th in Freiburg.
Those who were killed in Rastatt all came from the prison"

This had already been confirmed to Barkworth in Karl Buck's statement of 22nd September 1945:

"I know that 10 English and Americans were killed at Gaggenau. I also know that special execution commandos under Gehrum were touring the camps at that time, therefore if the English and Americans had not been shot on my orders, they would have been shot by Gehrum's"

In late August Lord Russell of Liverpool, deputy Judge Advocate General to B.A.O.R. wrote summarising the position to Sir Charles Knightley, General Officer, Commanding-in-Chief B.A.O.R.

Military Court (War Crimes) trial: General Seeger and 5 others

"All the accused pleaded not guilty and all were found guilty with the exception of Gehrum. All were alleged to be engaged in operating a system of extermination of 32 soldiers of 2 SAS Regiment who took part in 2 operations to disrupt enemy communications in the Vosges Mountains in August and September 1944.

At about this time there was a plan in existence known as "Action Waldfest" for the suppression of resistance forces. Schirmeck Camp was in the area controlled by the accused Schneider, assisted by Gehrum who moved

their headquarters from Strasbourg to Schirmeck Camp personally to direct the operation.

It was not alleged by the prosecution that any of these accused took any part in the actual killing of parachutists; the case against them was that these murders were the result of the orders they issued and decisions they made whilst occupying positions of authority in the organisation which carried out "Action Waldfest"

The shootings themselves were carried out by a party of thugs who took the victims into the woods, selected a suitable bomb crater to which they brought the prisoners of war stripped naked and then shot them one by one in the back of the neck the grave subsequently filled in and all trace of the killing removed. Many of these thugs have been tried and sentenced, the proceedings of their trials having been already confirmed by you.

All the parachutists whose deaths are the subject of the present charge were captured in uniform and made prisoners of war. All were shot without trial and there can therefore be no question of their having been legally executed,

It was in my opinion satisfactorily proved to the court that members of 2 SAS Regiment were killed in this way and that their killing was contrary to the laws and usages of war.

It was also satisfactorily proved in my opinion that the five accused who were convicted were all concerned in varying degrees with the death of at least some of these soldiers.

Before any sentence of death is carried out these proceedings must, after confirmation by you, be referred for his decision to C-in-C Germany who has power under Regulation 12 (War Crimes) to commute such sentences.

Brigadier: Russell of Liverpool DJAG

In late July 1946 Major-General A. G. M. Harris Chief of Staff at BAOR wrote to the British Military Mission to France confirming that on 3rd August 14 convicted War Criminals would be handed over to French Commandant Jadin at Strasbourg (having been tried by the British for the Vosges killings), for further trials in the killing of 4 French nationals at Gaggenau and elsewhere. Isselhorst and Schneider were not on that list, as Isselhorst was wanted at the Nuremburg Trials and despite

58

having already received a death sentence from the British, was still wanted by them in another trial.

In October 1946 British War Crimes Section were asked by their French counterparts to confirm to them, the sentences of six of the Germans tried in May at Wuppertal. Five were given the death sentence, but as Captain Young was at pains to point out in his reply all six sentences were *"still subject to confirmation"*. This was also true of the other eight criminals already handed over to the French.

Here was the kernel of the problem which was to come back to haunt the British War Crimes Group. In a memo dated 27th February 1947 Group Captain Somerhough i/c War Crimes Group pointed out the significant difference between the British and French legal procedure.

> *"As you are aware British Courts do not pronounce a judgement in the same way as Continental courts. They merely pronounce a verdict as to the accused being guilty or nor guilty of the charge upon which that accused is tried"*

On the 23rd of January 1947 Wilhelm Schneider was executed at Hameln Prison.

Eight months after their last unsuccessful request, on the 6th February 1947, the French War Crimes Liaison group wrote to War Crimes group NW Europe.

> *"Please be advised that the French Government has the highest interest to see Isselhorst handed over to France.*
> *Isselhorst has been head of the SD and SIPO in Strasbourg and is on that account the author of the execution of many members of the underground team "Alliance".*
> *Moreover he will be tried by a military court for these crimes, and he is wanted as a witness in many other cases. It is understood that if the sentence passed on him is lower than death, he will be rehanded to you"*

War Crimes Group NW Europe passed this request to D.J.A.G HQ with an attached comment.

12th February 1947

"As you know Isselhorst is giving evidence in the forthcoming SAS trials at Wuppertal.

This request amounts to an application that Isselhorst who is under sentence of death passed by a British Court, be handed over to the French for:

a) Trial by French Court

b) As a witness in French cases which are pending

c) Is also wanted by US authorities.

The matter seems to be one for the Army Commander to decide, and I have told the French that they should address further correspondence to you".

Meanwhile appeals for clemency for Dr. Isselhorst were being dealt with by DJAG. In March 1947 Brigadier Lord Russell of Liverpool wrote to General Officer Commanding BAOR:

"Attached is another letter from Cardinal Frings; this time invoking, on behalf of Isselhorst, "the highest right, which was instituted in kings by God" namely forgiveness and mercy

Isselhorst was the head of the Gestapo in the Strasbourg district and was responsible for the killing of a large number of British parachutists.

He is wanted by the French on a capital charge and the only reason he has not been hanged is that he has been used to get further information about Stalag Luft III; and is giving evidence at a War Crimes trial in Wuppertal at this moment.

The C-in-C Germany concurred in the death sentence in January of this year and dismissed the petition.

The letter from Cardinal Frings, who knows nothing about the case, discloses no grounds for interfering with the sentence."

Eventually Isselhorst was handed over to the French, tried, found guilty and on February 23rd 1948 he was executed by a French firing squad.

On the 16th of August 1947 the French held a ceremony at the bomb crater in Erlich Forest where the Gaggenau murders took place, to unveil a memorial to those killed there. Sadly it was redolent of previous French incompetence as it was held at very short notice with very few invitees. The Head of the French War Crimes Commission, General Furby wrote a letter of protest. Eventually on 20th October Major Eric Barkworth received this letter from Group Captain Somerhough O/C War Crimes Group:

> *"I enclose herewith some photographs and newspaper accounts of the Gaggenau ceremony which I attended. I also enclose a letter from General Furby protesting to the French authorities that proper notice had not been given to enable a detachment of the 2nd SAS to attend.*
> *Will you forward these to the Officer Commanding 2 SAS and explain that I, myself was only notified late on the evening before the ceremony and that I attended with Major Colthurst and Major Rivers-Berkeley of the Military Mission and the French Head of War Crimes General Furby.*
> *Had it been possible, I would have got you down here, but in view of the notice given me, nothing could be done"*

Major Barkworth must have felt snubbed and saddened not to have been given the chance to pay his respects to his fallen comrades.

In the summer of 1948 disaster struck. The Deputy Judge Advocate General's office at B.A.O.R. HQ discovered a critical legal error in the case of 14 of those convicted of the SAS murders, then handed over to the French. On the 13th September 1948, just over four years after team "Loyton" and team "Jacob" parachuted into the Vosges, Lt.General Sir Charles Knightley was obliged to explain this mistake to the Military Governor and C-in C, British Zone of Germany.

> *"The above named War Criminals were tried by Military Courts, under the Royal Warrant for the Trial of War Criminals, for the crimes set out against their names in the schedule attached, and were sentenced to death.*
> *As these accused were wanted by the French for war crimes committed in France, and some of them were only loaned to us by the French for the purpose of trial, with an undertaking that they would be handed back after trial, they were, <u>before</u> the findings and sentences of the Court could be promulgated to them, handed back to the French.*
> *The findings and sentences of the Courts were confirmed by my predecessor, and were concurred in by your predecessor, but for some reason which I have*

not been able to ascertain, owing to changes of staff, and re-organisation of War Crimes Trials, the findings and sentences of the Courts were not promulgated to the accused.

Consequently, promulgation is not complete, nor do the accused know whether the proceedings against them have, in fact, been confirmed

Three of these men have been under sentence of death for two years, another for over a year. In my view, it would now be contrary to both British and natural justice for their sentences to be carried out.

I therefore would ask your concurrence in the commutation of these sentences to imprisonment for life. If you agree with me, would you sign the attached minutes of commutation?"

By virtue of this procedural howler a number of those who gave the orders and those such as Ostertag and Ullrich who actually pulled the triggers at the Gaggenau murders had escaped their British executioner. Four days later DJAG received the following brief note from the Military Governor of the British Zone of Germany.

"With reference to the Army Commander's letter of 13th September, I enclose the minutes of commutation signed by the Military Governor.
The Military Governor regards it as reprehensible that a muddle should be possible on such a matter"

Major Barkworth of 2 SAS, who had worked so tirelessly to bring these criminals to account, must have been heartbroken. Since all the British "Wuppertal" death sentences had been commuted, due to the blunder of "non promulgation" there was now no way these particular war criminals would find their way back into British jurisdiction, as the three Allies had clearly agreed at the outset, that, whichever country handed down lawful death sentences, they would supersede any custodial punishments accrued elsewhere, and therefore that country would retain the convicted for execution.

The Gaggenau case like many other War Crimes prosecutions was complex partly because the victims were from three different Allied countries. In April 1947 after a trial at Rastatt the French War Crime Commission confirmed the death sentence on the six Germans previously tried by Britain at Wuppertal in May 1946.In the same letter however they announced that these six Germans were now being handed over to a French Military Court at Strasbourg for yet another trial After that of course the Americans would be waiting their turn to try these men for the murders of the four US Aircrew at Gaggenau, and so the grim legal merry-go-round continued turning. The commandant of Schirmeck Karl Buck whose 1946 British death sentence had been commuted because of the "non promulgation" fiasco, was by the early 1950's still "doing the rounds" of War Crime Trials. At a French Court in Metz he received the death sentence for 78 murders as well as ill treating prisoners at Schirmeck including, beating prisoners with his wooden leg, setting guard dogs on prisoners, ordering women prisoners to undress before him and forcing them to take ice cold showers, burying Alsace men up to their necks and threatening to decapitate them with a scythe. Three of his guards also received the death penalty and eight more terms of imprisonment of 5 to 20 years.

Rumours abounded that, behind the scenes Barkworth was also operating a secret "hit squad" of SAS personnel whose task was to liquidate a number of Gestapo thugs. In December 1997 "The Sunday Times" carried an article about Peter Mason, who claimed he was one of the hit men who operated under Barkworth's control from May 1945 to 1948.

Major Eric Barkworth and his War Crimes team were not universally popular within the British Military Establishment but their achievement in bringing to justice many of those responsible for the murders of SAS colleagues was remarkable.

SGT KENNETH SEYMOUR

Sgt. Kenneth Seymour was only 23 years old when he was captured on 17th August 1944. He spent no more than about 36 hours at Schirmeck camp before being transferred to the Gestapo at Strasbourg. According to his 1945 Secret de-brief report he was kept in a jail in Strasbourg for 10 days and was interrogated by two Gestapo men who claimed to have lived in London before the war and spoke excellent English. During this time he was fed on two bowls of soup per day and a small amount of bread. He contracted both scabies and impetigo, neither of which was treated by his captors.

He was then moved to an airbase at Hagenau where he was again kept in solitary but his diet improved. He was questioned by the Commandant and after 8 days, together with the entire crew of an American B-17 was taken to what he describes as an "interrogation" camp at Oberussel. Here he says they seemed to know something about British Special Forces. Again Seymour was kept in solitary confinement. He and his American companions were then despatched to Wetzlar which he described as a "transit" camp. On route they had the misfortune to be caught in an Allied bombing raid at Karlsruhre railway station, which experience he recalls in his de-brief report:

"During this journey we travelled in a train where we had to change at Karlsruhre station. As we approached the station an air-raid siren went off and they put us in one of the deep shelters near the station. After 2 hours when we emerged we found the place practically flattened and in flames, with numerous delayed action bombs going off.

As the railway line had been damaged we were forced to march about 4 miles to the next station. I was still without a shoe for my left foot. The population appeared to be much upset as a result of the raid, with women in hysterics. They apparently got the idea that we were part of the crews shot down during the raid. Persons passing by on bicycles struck us, men on the pavements made rushes at us between the guards, one in particular putting his arm around an American airman's neck and hammering his face with his fists.

During this march people threw stones at us and anything they could lay their hands on. I was hit by a brick but my head must have been very hard as the brick broke.

The cyclists bicycled ahead to warn people we were coming and by the time we reached the middle of the town they were ready to lynch us if they had got hold of us.

Our guards consisted of 2 Luftwaffe personnel armed with Schmeissers. Certain German Officers and men who were in the streets attached themselves to us and saw us through to the railway station. Had it not been for the action of these military personnel I am sure we would not have reached the station alive."

On arrival at Wetzlar, Seymour reported to the camp hospital where he spent five weeks in bed. They were unable to treat his damaged foot because, sadly, there was no X-Ray equipment to discover precisely what the injury was. He was treated for impetigo and well fed.

After 6 weeks there, Seymour was moved on to Limburg.

"I was taken to a chateau at Dites and held in solitary confinement and 2 days later was taken before a German Army Interrogation Officer. He asked me the usual questions but would not believe any of my answers. After 4 days of solitary I was moved to Stalag 8C at Sagan

Seymour describes the conditions at Sagan.

"This camp had been used mainly for French prisoners and there was not sufficient accommodation for the numbers involved. There were 4 huts in the British compound and when we arrived they housed 1200 men. There were not sufficient bunks to go round and many men had to double up. The German rations were then fairly reasonable. I stayed at Sagan until the middle of February 1945. We could hear the shelling of Russian guns and food got increasingly bad. Some days no bread at all, and when we did get bread it was only a 12th of a loaf, about 100 grams."

Seymour was soon to become part of the infamous "death marches" as the Germans retreated and took their prisoners with them. His report tells the story:

> *"One morning with no warning we were woken at 05.00 hours and told to pack and prepare to march to a new camp. We were told we should march for four days and then continue by train – in fact we marched for 42 days. For the first week we slept in the open in the snow with no blankets. Quite a number died – at the beginning from cold and later from dysentery and towards the end of the march from starvation. Eventually we arrived at Stalag 9C at Bad Orb by this time every man was very weak and suffering from malnutrition, the majority were also suffering from dysentery of which I was one, many also suffered from frostbite which attacked them on the first week of the march. Men were still dying in the camp hospital and the British M.O. could do nothing to help them owing to the shortage of food and medical supplies.*
>
> *On the 1st April the German Commandant decided to hand over the camp to the British prisoners, the German guards marched out of the camp, leaving it in our hands.*
>
> *The next morning the Americans arrived. By this time I was in hospital again and on 3rd April I was taken to a transit station and from Mainz I was flown to England to recover at Connaught Military Hospital in Surrey."*

On his return to England following repatriation, Sgt. Kenneth Seymour wrote to SFHQ from his hospital ward on 10th April 1945 to ask what had happened to Captain Gough and Lt.Baraud, and to query his pay records. On 13th April Lt.Colonel Carleton-Smith (DR/JED) at SFHQ replied with the news that Baraud was dead, and Gough was last seen at a concentration camp in Alsace towards the middle of November 1944. In this reply Seymour was ordered to submit a report on what had happened to him in France from the time of his landing until his release from captivity. He was instructed on no account to show it to anyone before returning it to Carleton-Smith in a sealed envelope marked "Top Secret". This he did shortly after April 1945.

At 5pm on May 12th 1945 Col. Carleton-Smith's secretary at SFHQ took a telephone message which she then typed for him to read the following morning:

> *To: Col. Carleton-Smith*   *From: SAS section (Capt. Reid)*
>
> *Sgt. Seymour*
>
> *SAS Section are very anxious to interview the above named NCO in connection with SAS personnel who were on the same Operation when above named was captured.*
>
> *Informed SAS that Sgt. Seymour will be coming in during the next few days and we will send him down to them.*

Since Seymour was not a member of 2 SAS, it would be interesting to know who told them, he was alive and recuperating at Connaught Hospital in Surrey.

By early June Major Barkworth of 2 SAS had begun his war crime investigations and within 12 months Seymour would be standing in the witness box of a War Crime Trial in Wuppertal appearing, incredibly, as a defence witness for Wilhelm Schneider. A curiosity of Seymour's Army Records is that on or about 21st September 1945 he was transferred to 2 SAS Regiment until November 6th when he was returned to RAC.

There are some odd contradictions in Seymour's "Top Secret" report of spring 1945, and in what he would later say in court in June 1946, when contrasted with what others, both British and German maintained. On page 1 of his report he says of his landing on August 13th 1944:

> *"unfortunately I seriously damaged the big toe of my left foot which necessitated my moving about without a shoe and the effects of which I still feel"….*

On page 2 of the report he recounts his capture on 17th August 1944 …

> " *I was carrying a shoe to ease my injured toe, they threw this away and when I tried to explain I wanted the shoe, they replied, I should not require it as I was to be shot*"...

Prior to his capture Seymour says he resisted as follows.

> ....." *The enemy started to attack whereupon the Maquisards abandoned their arms and equipment and fled down the mountain side. That left me alone as owing to the twisted nature of the path, I could not see what was happening at the head of the column. I took cover behind a jutting out portion of rock and opened fire with my Bren gun and when the ammunition was finished I took my carbine and then when the ammunition for that was finished I used my revolver.*".......

Major Barkworth's report suggested that at the time Seymour, because of his foot injury, was actually being carried on a make shift stretcher by the Maquis which they abandoned when the attack started. How he was capable of carrying a Bren gun plus his usual weapons and his radio set, in that condition is not explained. Wilhelm Schneider did say under oath that Seymour was very angry at being abandoned by his comrades. Captain Henry Druce commanding SAS Team "Loyton" "recce" party, from his home in Canada sent me a copy of an SAS report on the attack, and against the notes about Seymour, Druce wrote in his own hand "*He never fired a shot*"...

On page 2 of Seymour's report immediately after he ran out of ammunition he claims

> "*I dived into a sort of cave mouth and destroyed my papers, wireless plan, and crystals by burning them*"....

Another Jedburgh radio operator Ron Brierley to whom I spoke, told me it would need a very fierce fire indeed to destroy radio crystals, a better method would have been to crush them with the butt of a weapon. Having "destroyed" his papers, he was captured and a few lines further down page 2 of his report he says

"I was taken before a young officer who searched me; they took everything I had, leaving me with my battle dress only"

He then describes how he was taken back to their base about 3 miles from where he was captured.

"10 minutes later I was put in a sidecar and taken to an SS H.Q. about six miles away. They asked me for my full particulars, number, rank, name, and took my AB64 from me"….

Earlier on the same page, Seymour tells of destroying his papers, but now we discover he still has his pay book. His failure to destroy his AB64 pay book was a serious error for it could also have contained details of any courses he had been on and any qualifications, so it is possible that his captors already had proof of him being both a parachutist and a wireless operator.

Further down page 2 of Seymour's de-brief he writes:

"I did not let them know that we were there for sabotage nor did they know I was a wireless operator. He asked me what the S.F. (Special Forces) Badge was that I was wearing. I told him it was a paratroops badge."

But in Wuppertal in 1946 at Schneider's trial, when asked, Seymour says he could not remember if he had stripped off his insignia before capture, but if he had not, he was sure he was wearing RAC insignia.

On page 3 of his report Seymour writes:

"On arrival at Schirmeck Camp I was placed on a chair just inside the camp. At about 15.00 hours I was taken for further interrogation. The same questions were put to me, and a typist took down the answers and the questions."

Yet at Wuppertal in 1946 in the witness box the President of the Court pressed Seymour on several issues, including this:

Q. Answer my question a little more definitely, I asked you whether you got the impression that your answers were being taken straight down on to the typewriter.
A. No she was not taking down answers on the typewriter.

Both in his 1945 report and at Schneider's War Crime trial, Seymour denies that he told the Gestapo he was a wireless operator. On page 3 of Seymour's report he writes:

"*They then placed in front of me a Jedburgh one time pad, the silk and a Jedburgh transmitter set. I could not understand where they had come from, until they showed me a battle-dress blouse and asked if it was mine. I discovered it belonged to an SAS Captain. He had apparently very carelessly left all his papers in his blouse which he had discarded. I expressed complete ignorance of these papers and then they asked me if I knew anything about the transmitter. I replied I knew nothing about wireless*"

Kriminalrat M.A.Uhring in a sworn statement dated 20th November 1945 said:

"*With reference to the wireless operator who Schneider told me was taken prisoner between the middle and end of August, Schneider told me the wireless operator had "talked". I do know Schneider told me that the captured wireless operator had shown how to work the wireless set and the cipher*".

This is significant, since the only other British parachutists captured at that time, Davis and Hall of SAS Team "Loyton" were summarily murdered within hours of capture. So "the wireless operator" had to be Kenneth Seymour. The third member of the "triumvirate" Julius Gehrum in his sworn statement of 22nd November 1945 said:

"*I was also present during the interrogation of the first prisoner with the injured foot I noticed that the prisoner with the injured foot answered Schneider's questions, and Schneider said to me afterwards; with this man we can begin something...*"

In Major Barkworth's 1946 report for 2 SAS "Missing Parachutists", of which Seymour would have had no knowledge, Barkworth writes that Wilhelm Schneider claimed Seymour was not reluctant to give information unlike the next two prisoners taken, SAS Trooper Hall captured on the same day as Seymour, and Trooper Davis. In a sworn statement on 14th November 1945 given to Major Barkworth, Schneider recounts his interview with Sgt. Seymour.

"The following morning (19th August) I interrogated Seymour. I informed him of the provision by which soldiers found with the Maquis were liable to suffer the same fate as francs tireurs. He was visibly shaken, but when I told him that he would not be shot at once, he softened up and answered my questions. He told me of the light signals which were placed out for receiving the aircraft which brought resupply. These were to be placed in a triangle, with a longer point than the base. He said that there would be a twenty minute interval between planes. He told me too of the light signals to be made up to the aircraft. We tried this out, and made light signals to low flying aircraft which came over. Five or six times we found groups of excellently packed containers and many parachutes of wonderful silk. He told me that SAS stood for Special Air Service Regiment and that its members were given special training near London. He said he had come with a party in two aircraft – four or five men in each plane. Three wireless sets were brought to the camp. Only one was in working order, but the crystals were missing.

Seymour's attitude – I said to myself "now that the man has gone so far, he will tell us that too" – led me to form the opinion that we could use him to work it for us. We wanted to try to establish communications with England, and as we knew the light signals we hoped to make a big catch.

I spoke to Isselhorst on his return from Berlin and mentioned my plan to use the lights and the radio and Seymour's co-operative attitude"

Twice he was interrogated by Schneider who spoke English and once by Uhring with the help of the English speaking Professor Galinski of Strasbourg University. Seymour was to spend only about 36hours at Schirmeck Camp before being returned to the Gestapo in Strasbourg for further questioning.

The last two lines of Marie-Alphonse Uhring's sworn statement in 1945 affords us a possible explanation for Seymour's survival until the end of the war, Uhring stated.

"The wireless operator would only have been given to Kieffer, if Kieffer wished to make use of him"...

SS. Sturmbannfuhrer Hans-Josef Kieffer of the SD was possibly the most effective "spy-catcher" in France. SOE's clandestine activities in the Paris area had been successfully infiltrated in 1943. Kieffer was a key player in compromising some of their F Section circuits. It was Kieffer who held, for some months, SOE's agent Noor Inyat Khan (codenamed Madeleine) in 1943. He had agents planted in Resistance groups allowing him to arrest SOE parachutists as they landed at DZ's, including the "Bricklayer" team in February 1944.It was a Kieffer led operation that successfully ambushed 1 SAS Team "Gain" on their drop-zone at La Ferte-Alais in July 1944. Major Barkworth's report notes that in August 1944 there was a unit of Abwehr III F Section run by Kieffer, stationed at Chateau Scheideck in Lutzelhausen not more than 30 minutes drive from Schirmeck. It would be no surprise that Kieffer should take an interest in a captured SOE wireless operator, especially with Wilhelm Schneider's prediction to Julius Gehrum. *'With this man we can begin something"....*

Schneider went into the witness box at Wuppertal on June 24th 1946, during his examination he was questioned by Major Hunt the Chief Prosecutor for JAG 21st Army Group

Q. Three parachutists were brought into Schirmeck about the middle of August; that is right is it not?
A. the first two, later on one, three altogether.
Q. I suggest to you that you must know perfectly well which they were and what their names were. Just try and recollect. Seymour is alive today is he not?
A. I have heard about that
Q. Have you seen him?
A. No

Q. Do you say Seymour was the first, second, or third to be captured?

A. Seymour was one of the first to be.

Q. I suggest you know perfectly well. Was he the first or second or did they come together?

A. The prisoners Hall and Seymour came together and Seymour was wounded in the foot.

Q. You are quite clear about that are you?

A. Yes

Q. Then the third one to come was Davis; is that right?

A. Yes

Q. You interrogated Seymour did you not?

A. Yes

Q. And you thought you could get something out of Seymour did you not?

A. Yes

Q. And you have said you did get something out of Seymour, have you not?

A. Yes

Q. And unless you are lying, you got some very important information out of Seymour did you not?

A. It was very important at the time.

Q. And it was military information, was it not?

A, Yes

Q. Seymour was not shot was he?

A. No

Q. Davis refused to say anything, did he not?

A. Davis only gave me his name: otherwise nothing.

Q. And Davis was shot was he not?

A. As I heard later

Q. Did you get anything out of Hall?

A. No

Q. Would he not talk either?

A. No

Q. And he was shot too, was he not?

A. That I also heard later on, but I had nothing to do with it.

Q. Do you know why Seymour was not shot?

A. No

Q. Were you satisfied that Seymour had been working with the Maquis just as much as, say, Davis or Hall?

A. Seymour had been found in the Maquis Headquarters with a wounded foot and he was taken prisoner there, and he was very annoyed that they had left the camp – they just left him lying there in his helpless state.

Q. Did you hear anything about the connection between the paratroops and the Maquis?

A. Yes, I heard about it through the statement of Seymour, and also in the headquarters south-east of Raon-sur-Plaine we found eighty thousand small arms ammunition, machine guns, machine pistols medical equipment and so on.

Q. Was there not a very good case for shooting Seymour because he had been with the Maquis?

A. At that time there was no talk about shootings. After all I had an order to keep prisoners in custody until the return of the B.D.S. (Dr.Isselhorst)

Later in Schneider's trial (25th June 1946) Seymour was cross examined on this matter by Major Hunt Prosecuting Counsel.

Q. You have just said you were interrogated by the accused Schneider; did he interrogate you in English?

A. Yes, I was asked in English

Q. How did he start the interrogation?

A. I cannot remember that.

Q. Did he ask you your name, rank, and number and so forth?

A. My name and everything they took from my pay book.

Q. at some period in this interrogation presumably you objected to answering questions, is that right?

A. That is correct.

Q. When they found they could not get the answers they wanted, were you threatened, and, if so, in what manner?

A. I never remember being threatened directly – that is with a direct order.

Q. Were you told that if you did not talk you would be shot?

A. Indirectly, yes, they did say that.

Q. Did you as a result answer the questions?

A. Two questions I gave them answers to, but both completely untrue.

Q. What were they?

A. One question was about our landing lights and the other was the number of men we had with us.

Q. How many men did you say you had with you?

A. The question depends on whether we count those SAS and Maquis as well. The number I said was six.

Q. And was the answer about the landing lights also untrue?

A. Absolutely untrue.

Q. If you believed you were going to be shot was it not a bit dangerous to give untrue information?

A. No, there were only two choices, one was to be a traitor and the other was to bluff; and I used bluff.

Q. Supposing you in fact refused to answer the questions at all, as others did, what would happen then?

A. I do not know.

Q. Have you read Schneider's account of his interrogation of you?

A. No not a complete account; I have seen about two points concerning it.

Q. Is Schneider's account true or is yours?

A. The only point I agree with is his question of asking me about the lights.

Q. Otherwise is Schneider's report of your interrogation, to put it at its lowest, exaggerated?

A. Yes

Q. You mean you do not admit what Schneider said about you?

A. No I do not.

Q. Were Davis and Hall some of the party that were rendezvousing in France with you?

A. Yes, I think they were

Q. And had they any more to do with the Maquis than you did?

A. No

Q. Do you know that they had been shot?

A. Yes

Q. You cannot give any reason why you were not shot, can you?

A. None at all. My only thought about it is that I was the first to be captured.

Q. I am a little puzzled. You gave false information you say, to the Germans?

A. Yes

Q. The Germans themselves say that Davis would not give any information at all. You cannot think of any reason why you should have escaped being shot and Davis should be shot?

76

A. The only reason is that when I was taken to Haggenau, Haggenau was Luftwaffe and I came to the conclusion that nobody knew exactly what my job was and I was taken as being something to do with the RAF.

Q. What made you say anything at all? Was it because you had been threatened or why?

A. I do not really know.

Q. You could have said nothing of course, could you not?

A. Yes

Q. did you think it was a half way house to give them false information, is that your idea?

A. Yes, I should say it was.

Q. And at any rate it would put off the shooting date for some time, is that the idea?

A. Well, I was just trying to be optimistic.

Q. You say what you told the Germans was untrue about the landing lights, is that right?

A. Yes

Q. Did nobody come to you and tell you they had tried the information?

A. No, nobody at all.

Q. – That they had tried the information that you had given and that they had no luck in capturing parachute troops?

A. No, nobody came to see me at all.

Q. So it seems pretty clear that the Germans did not find that you had been telling lies, is that right?

A. I suppose so.

Q. But I think you have rather given the court, you know, the picture of a man interrogating you who really is not using threats to you at all; I was wondering whether that was a true picture?

A. Well, it is difficult to remember these little things. It is nearly two years. At that time I did not worry about what anybody looked like or took any notice what people were saying.

Q Did you get the impression from him that he would have you shot if you did not give him the answers he wanted?

A. I had that impression.

What remains very curious is why Seymour appeared at all at Schneider's Trial in Wuppertal. During Schneider's examination in court, his counsel Dr.Luedecke asked if he might call a repatriated soldier not already listed as a witness. Major Hunt Prosecutor for JAG said he was very willing to arrange this, however the Judge Advocate (Mr.G.L.Stirling K.C.) interrupted to make it very clear to the Court, the rules in this matter:

> *"They cannot be made to come. It is just a question of whether they will come. We have no authority to make people come, and the most the British authorities can do is to say to somebody: "Will you go to Germany and give evidence?" If they say "Yes," then they will go. If they say" No" then we have no power to make them go".*

So, on the face of it Seymour was not obliged to attend as a witness for the defence, he could have refused. Either he went because he believed he was innocent of any suggestions of aiding the enemy, contrary to what German witnesses were insisting and Major Barkworth was implying, or had he been given some kind of ultimatum by Special Forces? Maybe his temporary transfer to 2 SAS in the autumn of 1945 (as shown in his Army record) had something to do with it? Perhaps it had been suggested to him "take your chances in court at Wuppertal and let's see if people believe your story, or face charges of giving information useful to an enemy."

What is certain is that, briefly, Seymour was in the spotlight, for the day after his appearance in Court at Schneider's trial in Wuppertal, his picture and a news story about his part in the Vosges operation appeared on the front page of "The Daily Herald" newspaper. On Thursday July 4th 1946 a longer article on Seymour appeared on page one of his local paper the "Sutton Times & Cheam Mail". The headline in the "Sutton Times" was eye-catching, ***Man with "Talk Or Be Shot" Choice.*** In this interview Seymour repeated his epic fight sequence (as mentioned in his SOE de-brief report) with a large German force armed with machine guns and hand grenades and how he fired a Bren gun, his carbine and pistol until his ammunition ran out. Curiously he is also quoted in this article as claiming they were dropped into the Vosges area a few days after the Allies landed in Normandy, when in fact they landed on the night of 12th/13th August. He is also quoted as saying:

"He was asked about his comrades and the code lights the Maquis flashed. Seymour thought fast, gave convincing answers, but not true. It was just bluff, he said, but it saved his life.

Further on in this article he claims to have been sent back to the Vosges to help investigate the murders of many other airborne men by the Germans. This would of course tie in with his temporary transfer to 2 SAS in the autumn of 1945

Kenneth Roy Seymour was born in October 1921 and had lived with his family in the same house in Lewis Road since birth. He attended Sutton County School and was apprenticed in the heating and lighting trade when he joined the Army in 1942. At the time of this press interview he was preparing to marry his sweetheart Pamela Vaughan from a well known Sutton family. On 19th July 1946 Seymour was officially discharged from the Army (he remained on the TA reserve list until 1951) and on July 26th they were married in their local church in Sutton. At much the same time as Seymour and his family were reading of his exploits in the "Sutton Times & Cheam Mail" the Judge Advocate General's office were making a case for the prosecution of Sgt. Seymour.

The Germans, particularly Wilhelm Schneider, in their interrogation statements and in evidence at court said, that Seymour told them about the following:

The SAS and where they were trained.
How to work the wireless set.
The use of ciphers for operating the wireless set.
The number of men and planes used in the first drop.
The number of radio sets they brought.
The landing lights and layout for a drop (which Seymour says was a bluff)

All SOE Jedburgh volunteers were required to read and sign the Official Secrets Act 1911 & 1920. If any of the claims made both by accused Germans and Major Barkworth are to be believed, the least we can say is that Sgt. Seymour was probably guilty of breaking the Official Secrets Act. What had he put his signature to? The relevant sections are these:

> *If any person:*
> *(a) Communicates the code word, pass word, sketch, plan, model, article, note, document, or information to any person, other than a person to whom he is authorised to communicate it to.*
> *(aa) uses the information in his possession for the benefit of any foreign power, or in any other manner prejudicial to the safety or interests of the State.*
> *(c) Fails to take reasonable care of, or so conducts himself as to endanger the safety of sketch, plan, model, article, note, document, secret official code, or pass word, or information:*
>
> *That person shall be guilty of a misdemeanour.*

What was the punishment for such a breach?

> *"Any person who is guilty of a misdemeanour under the Official Secrets Act shall be liable on conviction or indictment to imprisonment, with or without hard labour, for a term not exceeding two years., or on conviction under the Summary Jurisdiction Acts, to imprisonment, with or without hard labour, for a term not exceeding three months or to a fine not exceeding fifty pounds or both imprisonment and fine"*

It seems clear Seymour's appearance at the Wuppertal War Crime trial had not convinced the Judge Advocate General's office that his behaviour in captivity was acceptable. Even after being sentenced to hang, Wilhelm Schneider in his appeal petition continued to maintain:

> *"Seymour gave valuable information away and was transferred to Strasbourg where he was interrogated by Kriminal Commissar Callis"*

Schneider was to repeat his claim about Seymour yet again in a witness statement read out during Lt. General Willy Seeger's trial at Wuppertal in June 1946. This reflected the views of Major Barkworth who at the time he produced his "Missing Parachutists" report in late 1945, had also written a separate critical report on Seymour's conduct in captivity.

Telex messages from JAG HQ in Cockspur Street were sent to 21st Army Group BAOR. On the 12th July the following message was transmitted:

> "ACCUSED ISSELHORST AND SCHNEIDER / THESE ACCUSED SENTENCED TO DEATH WUPPERTAL 11 JULY / PROBABLY WANTED AS WITNESSES AGAINST SOLDIER FOR SERIOUS OFFENCE / ENSURE DEATH SENTENCE NOT EXECUTED WITHOUT REFERENCE THIS OFFICE"

At the end of July 1946, only weeks after Seymour had appeared in the witness box in Schneider's defence, Major-General A.J.M.Harris, Chief of Staff at BAOR H.Q. wrote to the British Military Mission for France advising them that 14 Germans convicted by the British for the Vosges murders of Special Forces, would on August 3rd be handed to Commandant Jadin at Strasbourg for the French War Crimes trials to begin. Two senior Gestapo men, Isselhorst and Schneider were not included in this transfer. In paragraph 5 of Major-General Harris's memo is the following very interesting comment:

> *"Isselhorst and Schneider are required as witnesses in person at a forthcoming British Court martial...."*

All contemporary documents refer to the prosecution of Germans as "Military Court (War Crimes) Trials", but a Court Martial implies that a member of the British Armed Forces was charged with a crime. Who connected with the Vosges Special Forces operations of 1944 might be the subject of a Court Martial? At whose trial would Isselhorst and Schneider be useful witnesses? Of the 98 Officers and men of Special Forces dropped into the Vosges area in late summer of 1944, 63 made their way safely through German lines, 2 were killed in action, and 33 taken prisoner, 32 of those prisoners were murdered in cold blood, the only survivor was Sgt. Kenneth Roy Seymour. Isselhorst and Schneider had quite clearly never encountered any of the 63 men who exfiltrated, so if it was one of those being Court Martialled, what use would Isselhorst and Schneider be at their trial? The only man with whom they had a connection, was, the sole survivor of captivity Sgt. Seymour, about whom Schneider claimed *"with this man we can begin something"*. On 27th August the following instruction was sent to the British Secretary at the International War Crime Tribunal in Nuremburg, where Isselhorst was appearing as a witness:

> "REQUEST IMMEDIATELY ISSELHORST AVAILABLE RE-COLLECTION AS WANTED IN UK FOR COURT MARTIAL"

On September 4th 1946 the following urgent message was sent from JAG.

> "HAVE REQUESTED DJAG TO INTERROGATE ISSELHORST AND SCHNEIDER IN BAOR AS POSSIBLE WITNESSES AGAINST SERJEANT K R SEYMOUR. REQUEST INTERROGATION ARRANGED SOONEST. WHEN INTERROGATION COMPLETED CAN DECIDE WHETHER REQUIRED AS WITNESSES AT TRIAL OF SEYMOUR IN ENGLAND"

On the 5th September a temporary transfer order was granted for Eric Isselhorst to be moved from Werl Prison to the Military Governor's Gaol at Wuppertal where he would again be interrogated on or around September 10th by Major Eric Barkworth.

Aside from the Official Secrets Act 1911 & 1920, the Judge Advocate General's office was almost certainly considering charging Seymour under the 1940 Treachery Act. Passed into law by Parliament in the same month that Hitler invaded the Low Countries and Winston Churchill became Prime Minister, this Act (unlike the Treason Act of 1351) had no requirement to prove allegiance to the Crown. To find someone guilty under the Treachery Act, all that is required is to show that the acts the accused committed, or intended to commit, would endanger the forces of the Crown including personnel as well as physical objects. These requirements are expressed in Section 1 of the Treachery Act:

If, with intent to help the enemy, any person does, or attempts or conspires with any other person to do any act which is designed or likely to give assistance to the naval, military or air operations of the enemy, to impede such operations of His Majesty's forces, or to endanger life, shall be guilty of felony and shall on conviction suffer death.

The dilemma for JAG was, could they prove that what Seymour might have done, conformed to the definition of the Treachery Act. Furthermore since their key witnesses were Gestapo men, Isselhorst and Schneider, both under the death sentence, would their evidence stand up under scrutiny and cross examination? Now in late 1946, with the war over and Britain struggling with a period of austerity, was there the appetite to follow through with the prosecution of Sergeant Seymour?

There is nothing in Seymour's Army Record to indicate any conviction or sentence, having been demobbed in July 1946 he remained on the reserve list until 1951, not a plausible proposition for any soldier who had been on trial for a serious crime.

At this time no further evidence has come to light to show if JAG did take Seymour to trial, or why they might have abandoned their case. I have been reminded by the Ministry of Defence of just how little World War II material has survived in the National Archives. Their Historical Branch suggested that as little as 10% of all documentation still remains on file. We may never discover the full story behind the tragic events in the Vosges in 1944.

EPILOGUE

**"It is not a matter of conserving some ashes,
It is a matter of preserving the flame"**
(quotation from French Resistance Memorial)

Captain Gough was posthumously awarded the Croix de Guerre with Silver Star by French General Order No.229 on the 12th March 1945, and on 30th August 1945 he was mentioned in Despatches in the London Gazette.

On October 29th 1945 Captain Gough's next of kin Mrs. K. Baird wrote to Captain Dalton at Special Forces HQ.

> *"Thank you for sending me the letter from Col. Franks. Capt. Buck wrote to me some months ago and stated you would be writing to me about the late Capt. Gough's Croix de Guerre decoration which I very much want to have. Have you any idea what has happened to his note case and signet ring, or do the Huns always steal their prisoner's personal belongings?"*

A month later Captain Dalton replied in part:

> *"I am afraid that I am not able to give you any information about the note-case and signet ring. We have had no articles of personal property returned to us by the German or French authorities and I am very much afraid that your suggestion is correct – that, in addition to the bestial treatment which the enemy meted out to their prisoners, they had no compunction, apparently, in stealing their personal property."*

For as long as I can remember my grandmother Marjorie Gough had a photograph of her son Captain Victor Gough in his uniform, on her mantelpiece. For as long as I can remember, she never spoke a word about him. It was only after her death we discovered that what we took to be a brooch, was in fact his Croix de Guerre medal with a pin welded on the back. There was no sign of the ribbon. It was only then that we discovered the actual citation was still waiting to be claimed from the War Office.

My mother, Vic's sister, always maintained that "Nanny" was very bitter about her daughter surviving the war, whilst Vic had lost his life. During the war my mother who worked at the Bristol Aeroplane Company at Filton, was of course in a place of potential danger, as the aircraft factory had been a Luftwaffe target. But it was not of course the same degree of danger, as dropping behind enemy lines. We knew little of his life, his short marriage, and of the mysterious Mrs. Baird with whom he lived in Somerset and who he had nominated as his next of kin. His SOE personnel file shows considerable correspondence between the War Office, my Grandmother and Mrs Baird over ownership of his effects and his medal. The War Office, whilst they sent his War Service Record to his Mother, were clear that the medal should go to Mrs. Baird but somewhere along the line; there must have been an accommodation between them, as clearly the medal ended up with Nanny.

The citation was finally obtained from the War Office and some research revealed the outline of his work with the Jedburghs in 1944 and his subsequent fate at Gaggenau. It has to be remembered that much of the material on SOE and the Jedburghs was at this time, still classified, some of it for as much as 75 years.

In the 1970's my parents moved from Somerset to Berkshire. Shortly after a former neighbour, who had been told something of Uncle Vic's war time activities, saw and recorded for them a TV documentary "The Secret Hunters" about the work of Major Barkworth's War Crime Investigation Team which had been shown on the local commercial channel in the West Country. Following a complicated chain of contacts via the then owner of the Castle Hotel Taunton (ex SAS), to the researcher on this TV programme Anthony Kemp, himself a writer on clandestine matters in WW II, my parents received a letter from Germany. It was from Werner Helfen, Captain Gough's fellow prisoner at Schirmeck, whom Anthony Kemp had met during the filming of this documentary in the Vosges and Strasbourg area. Devoid of German, my parents relied on a friend to translate Werner's letters.

Some months later they received a small parcel from Germany. Werner had sent some photographs of himself, one in his wartime uniform prior to his arrest in 1944, and another up to date one of him standing beside Uncle Vic's war grave at Durnbach Cemetery. His gravestone is simply inscribed "Captain Victor Gough, Somerset Light Infantry 25th November 1944". Also in the parcel was the silk escape map which Uncle Vic had given as a gift to Werner Helfen all those years ago at Schirmeck Camp, just days before the murders at Gaggenau.

After he left the Army Kenneth Seymour seemed to vanish into anonymity. One or two former Jeds believe he attended an early Jedburgh re-union, and a few recall there being some vague rumours about his wartime conduct and a least one Glyn Loosemore claims to have read the Daily Herald article about Seymour in 1946. Seymour married Pamela Vaughan and had four children. About a year after his marriage he enrolled at teacher training college and became a woodwork and technical drawing teacher and retired as a Head of Mathematics in Hertfordshire. He died in October 2004. The big toe he broke on landing in the Vosges in 1944 which was never properly treated whilst in captivity, remained blackened for the rest of his life.

In 1979 Seymour, then teaching Maths at Bessemer School, Hitchin, was persuaded by his pupils to write an article for the school magazine about his wartime experiences. Much of it followed the same pattern as his 1945 de-brief report for Lt.Colonel. Carleton-Smith (DR/JED). Several claims he made in this article for the school magazine were patently wrong. Even allowing for the fact that he wrote this account at the age of 58, 35 years after the event, he claims that they took off on June 7th 1944 for their mission, not August 13th (as shown on his Army Record form) exactly the same claim he made in the 1946 interview he gave to his local paper the "Sutton Times & Cheam Mail". He says he spent nearly a year at Milton Hall training. This cannot be true since SOE only took over Milton Hall in February 1944. In the few days before his capture he says they carried out three sabotage actions, none of which are reported in Captain Gough's radio messages, and in any case sabotage was not part of Team "Jacob's" brief. He says he was only able to contact London by radio, once. From transcripts of Captain

Gough's early messages Gough states he was using an SAS operator for the very reason that Seymour with his broken toe would not have been able to walk the five miles away from camp in order to send messages. He says he was told on the second day of his capture (August 18th 1944) that both Captain Gough and Lt.Baraud had been killed. Baraud was killed in action in early September and Gough was not murdered until 25th November, and just how did his captors know their names? He also says that all the SAS were killed and no trace of them was ever found, which is patently untrue, since he attended the trial for their murders, and every single body had been located and identified by the American and British war crimes teams. A footnote to this article declared it was the only time he wrote about or disclosed any details of his wartime activities.

Seymour was 23 years old when he was captured in the Vosges on 17th August 1944. If he did give information to the Gestapo, as they maintained, it was done no doubt out of fear, with self preservation in mind. How do we judge his conduct, when we ourselves could not know how we might behave in such circumstances? For the rest of his life he would have to live with his thoughts of that episode, and the memory of 32 captured comrades of Special Forces who kept silent and did not return home.

Postscript

Although the Jedburghs had no official post-war Association they did hold a substantial re-union in 1996. My Mother and I attended the Memorial Service in Peterborough Cathedral, just a few miles from their wartime base at Milton Hall, when a memorial plaque dedicated to the Jeds was unveiled. A similar plaque is to be found in the stable block at Milton Hall. At the Jedburgh Re-Union we met Clive Bassett an historian well versed in the wartime work of both the Jeds and OSS, the American counterpart of SOE. He is also a leading light at the "Carpetbaggers" Aviation Museum based at the former RAF Harrington in Northamptonshire, the wartime home of the American OSS operations. The Museum specialises in SOE, Jedburgh and OSS material. It is housed in the wartime "Ops" building and visitors can now see a substantial feature about Captain Victor Gough with photographs, (including of his friend Werner Helfen) his Croix de Guerre medal, and the same SOE escape map given to Werner Helfen in 1944 and returned to Gough's family nearly 50 years later.

SOURCES

NATIONAL ARCHIVES

WO 32/9392	WO 235/682
WO 218/209	WO 309/72
WO 218/219	WO 309/717
WO 218/222	WO 309/718
WO 219/2402A	WO 309/719
WO 219/2402B	WO 311/43
WO 235/185	HS 9/604/5
WO 235/554	HS 6/529
WO 235/558	HS 9/1348

UN War Crime Trials Vol.5 Case 29 HMSO 1948

"2 SAS War Crime Investigations"
Dr. L. Charlesworth (Journal of Intelligence History 2006)

War Diary SO Branch, OSS London Vol.4 "Jedburgh"

CIA Studies in Intelligence 1998/9 Robert.R.Kehoe
"An Allied Team with the Resistance"

Army Personnel Centre (Historical disclosures) Glasgow

SAS Regimental Association Archivist Grenville Bint

"Anything but a Soldier" by John Hislop. Michael Joseph 1965
Reproduced by kind permission of Mr. Ian Hislop (son)

"Secret War" by Nigel West. Hodder & Stoughton 1992

Private correspondence Major Henry Druce 2 SAS

Private correspondence Herr Werner Helfen

Daily Herald newspaper circa June 27th 1946

Sutton Times & Cheam Mail July 6th 1946

The Sunday Times December 28th 1997

Lightning Source UK Ltd.
Milton Keynes UK
05 December 2009

147146UK00002B/17/P